D1707777

A Day of Glory

A Shade of Vampire, Book 32

Bella Forrest

ALSO BY BELLA FORREST:

THE GENDER GAME

The Gender Game

A SHADE OF VAMPIRE SERIES:

Series 1:
Derek & Sofia's story:

A Shade of Vampire (Book 1)
A Shade of Blood (Book 2)
A Castle of Sand (Book 3)
A Shadow of Light (Book 4)
A Blaze of Sun (Book 5)
A Gate of Night (Book 6)
A Break of Day (Book 7)

Series 2:
Rose & Caleb's story:

A Shade of Novak (Book 8)
A Bond of Blood (Book 9)
A Spell of Time (Book 10)
A Chase of Prey (Book 11)
A Shade of Doubt (Book 12)
A Turn of Tides (Book 13)
A Dawn of Strength (Book 14)
A Fall of Secrets (Book 15)
An End of Night (Book 16)

Series 3:
Ben & River's story:

A Wind of Change (Book 17)
A Trail of Echoes (Book 18)
A Soldier of Shadows (Book 19)
A Hero of Realms (Book 20)
A Vial of Life (Book 21)
A Fork Of Paths (Book 22)
A Flight of Souls (Book 23)
A Bridge of Stars (Book 24)

Series 4:
A Clan of Novaks

A Clan of Novaks (Book 25)
A World of New (Book 26)
A Web of Lies (Book 27)
A Touch of Truth (Book 28)
An Hour of Need (Book 29)
A Game of Risk (Book 30)
A Twist of Fates (Book 31)
A Day of Glory (Book 32)

A SHADE OF DRAGON:

A Shade of Dragon 1
A Shade of Dragon 2
A Shade of Dragon 3

A SHADE OF KIEV TRILOGY:

A Shade of Kiev 1

A Shade of Kiev 2

A Shade of Kiev 3

BEAUTIFUL MONSTER DUOLOGY:

Beautiful Monster 1

Beautiful Monster 2

For an updated list of Bella's books,
please visit www.bellaforrest.net

Join my VIP email list and I'll personally send you an email reminder as
soon as my next book is out!
Click here to sign up: www.forrestbooks.com

Contents

THE "NEW GENERATION" NAMES LIST

- **Arwen:** (daughter of Corrine and Ibrahim - witch)
- **Benedict:** (son of Rose and Caleb - human)
- **Brock:** (son of Kiev and Mona – half warlock)
- **Grace:** (daughter of Ben and River – half fae and half human)
- **Hazel:** (daughter of Rose and Caleb – human)
- **Heath:** (son of Jeriad and Sylvia – half dragon and half human)
- **Ruby:** (daughter of Claudia and Yuri – human)
- **Victoria:** (daughter of Vivienne and Xavier – human)

Bastien

I woke up to the feel of Victoria's bare body pressed against mine—her scent tantalizing my senses, her gentle breathing. As consciousness trickled through me, I remembered what had happened. I had made Victoria mine.

Imagining waking up like this with Victoria every day filled me with joy I'd never thought I would have a taste of.

I glanced down at her beautiful sleeping face, her lips slightly parted. I claimed those lips, drawing her awake alongside me.

Her eyes blinked open. It took her a few seconds to

focus… and then she was sharing my smile.

I was in such a daze, lost in my new mate, that it was only when she asked the time that reality came slamming back.

Oh, my.

Untwining from Victoria, I slid out of bed and hurried to the window. Judging by the position of the sun in the sky, hours had passed since we had first locked ourselves in here.

Yuraya.

My heart stopped beating as I remembered my cousin. Grabbing Victoria, I quickly pulled some clothes over her while wrapping a garment around my waist. Then I hurried with her to Yuraya's cabin at the bottom of the boat. The last time I had entered it, she was still unconscious, I had been in such a hurry to complete my bonding with Victoria that I could not remember whether I had left the door ajar or closed. Now, it was closed.

Having no idea how much time had passed, I had to hope that Cecil had remained alert to continue feeding her the weed.

But as I stepped inside, it was clear he hadn't.

The spot where Yuraya had been resting was empty. There was no trace of her anywhere in the room.

"Oh, no," Victoria gasped, her grip around my arm tightening.

Where is she?

Feeling more afraid for Victoria than ever, I hurried up the staircase, keeping her behind me. Reaching the sunny deck, I glanced around cautiously.

Noticing nothing immediately suspicious, I tentatively called out, "Cecil?"

No answer.

Oh, fates, don't let that woman have gotten to Cecil. No, no, no.

As we hurried to Cecil's control cabin, I was expecting to see his body a mangled mess… but it wasn't.

He was lying on the bench, taking a nap. Or rather, a deep sleep. He was snoring loudly.

I stared at him, then gripped his shoulders and shook him awake.

"Cecil!" I said, rousing the old man. "Yuraya! She's gone!"

"Wh-What?" He rubbed his eyes.

"How long have you been sleeping?" I asked him.

"I-I don't know," he said slowly, his brows knotting. "I was so tired. Once we had gotten a fair distance away from The Dunes I felt unbearably sleepy. I had not slept properly in a long time."

This was the absolute worst time that he could've picked to sleep, but I could hardly lay any blame on him. *I* should not have fallen asleep. But our bonding had been more

3

exhausting than I had thought it might be. It had tired me out, body, mind and soul. Both Victoria and I couldn't help but fall into slumber, losing consciousness before we had even realized it.

"So what now?" Victoria whispered.

Still holding her hand, I raced to the other end of the deck and glanced down at the balcony, just in case Yuraya might've been hiding there for some reason. She wasn't.

Then we headed back down to the lower decks and searched every cabin thoroughly, fearing she might be playing a game of hide-and-seek.

She wasn't.

She was nowhere on the boat.

She had just... vanished.

The most surprising thing about all of this was that Victoria was still alive. Or that I was, for that matter. Surely, after waking from her stupor, Yuraya would have searched the ship. She must've seen Victoria and me lying naked in each other's arms. I could only imagine what that would have done to her.

She should have been seething. Ready to rip us both to shreds.

But she hadn't. She had gone.

"What could've happened?" Victoria asked, gazing at me wide-eyed.

4

I exhaled a breath. "I don't know," I replied.

Though something told me we had definitely not seen the last of her…

MONA

There were a lot of worse places Brock and I could have been stuck waiting in the supernatural dimension. The Woodlands was beautiful, and it was a land that was fairly familiar to me, due to my prior involvement with the black witches. It wasn't difficult for Brock and me to locate fresh water and food to keep us going.

I also enjoyed the opportunity to have some quality time with my son. We were usually both so busy and often running in different directions, that time together was hard to come by. If only Kiev was here—then we could have called it a family outing. I guessed that he would be wrapped up in whatever the League's latest misadventures were.

Not that my husband was a picnic kind of guy. His old age had made him a typical man in that sense. When he wanted to relax, he liked the convenient, familiar surroundings of home.

As Brock and I sat perched on a branch, eating a snack of fleshy pink fruits, our pleasant conversation was interrupted by a chorus of shrieking. Shrieking that chilled me to the bone. That sort of shrieking wasn't something you heard from someone unless they were in severe pain, maybe even dying.

Dropping the fruit, Brock and I left the branch and hurtled in the direction of the noise. We soon realized that it was coming from Blackhall Mountain.

Arriving above the entrance, we found ourselves gazing down at a nightmarish scene. Giant black wolves were attacking a group of much smaller ones, who appeared to be trying to defend their lair.

Then I realized that they were not just attacking the Blackhalls... They were eating them.

"It's the Mortclaws," Brock said, his breath hitching. "*Now* do you believe that they are still cannibals?"

My voice caught in my throat. I had been reluctant to interfere with the Mortclaws until now because, first, their preference of wife for their son was a family affair, and second, I'd had no proof that they were still cannibals. But now that I saw this… abomination… I couldn't simply stand still and watch.

"Hey!" I roared down. The first thing I wanted to do was grab their attention, distract them from biting into those poor wolves.

But it didn't work. Only a few of them glanced up briefly before immediately stooping back down to their meals.

All right. If this is how you want to play things…

Mustering my power to my fingertips, I hovered down and began to freeze the Mortclaws one by one—attempting to catch them when their jaws were not closed around a victim. Brock assisted me, and once we had stunned every one of them—which included freezing their eyeballs—I looked to my son.

"You can help me now," I told him. "Let's line them all up at the edge of the woods."

Brock was quick to assist. Soon, every one of the Mortclaws lay in frozen positions by the trees. Though their limbs were stiff and immobile, I had let them retain use of their mouths and voices. They exploited their ability to speak to the maximum as they hurled insults and threats at me.

These folks really did not take kindly to interruptions at dinnertime.

Brock and I hurried to assist the injured Blackhalls,

healing as many as we could. But some, sadly, didn't make it. They passed away before we could assist them.

Poor Bastien. This was going to break his heart.

Assuming Victoria ever found him.

Once the Blackhalls were safely back inside their lair to recover from the trauma—their fallen taken in with them, presumably to hold some kind of funeral ceremony—Brock and I returned our attention to the monsters.

My son glanced at me, raising his brows. "So… what do we do with them now?" he asked.

I blew out. *That is a good question…*

YURAYA

My chest was on fire as I hurtled back to The Woodlands. Bastien. He had betrayed me. He had betrayed me in my most vulnerable state, just after I had expressed my love to him. Just after he had told me that he wanted me, too. I felt mortally wounded. My soul felt shattered. I didn't know how I would ever recover from this… but revenge was a good way to start.

It had been such a great temptation to tear at that hussy's throat the second I saw her naked form entwined in my betrothed's arms. I hated that I sensed a connection with the human girl, a pull deep inside me, toward her, as though she were a Mortclaw herself. But my mind was too turbulent to pay it much attention. She could have been my sister, and I'd still want to slit her throat.

I had detected an energy around the couple, almost an aura, that made me believe they had already bonded, even though I had not been there to witness it. *Bonded.* That meant that Bastien was tarnished. That he could never truly be mine.

Somehow or other, I had managed to hold myself back from murdering her then. This was a job best shared with Bastien's mother. I would fetch Sendira, and the two of us could mutilate her together. The experience would be far more satisfying for the both of us.

What was that man thinking, going against his mother's wishes?

Did Sendira not already warn him that if he ever saw that human again, the girl would incur the wrath of the entire Mortclaw tribe?

He must've lost his mind to see her again. Well, he would pay dearly for this transgression… if it was the last thing I did.

On reaching The Woodlands, I used my senses to locate my tribe. My brain had been telling me to head immediately for our home—our mountain lair—but my senses led me in a different direction. I soon realized that I was heading toward the Blackhalls' lair.

But arriving over the clearing in front of their mountain entrance, I stopped short.

My family. All of them. Paralyzed and lined up in a row. Before them stood a blonde woman and a young man. *Witches.*

I backed away, my heart pounding. I couldn't be seen or they might trap me too.

I hurried around the mountain, out of sight, and touched down on a rock to contemplate what my next move should be.

My family was in need—including my mother and father. But what could I do to help, all alone? I was no match for them, when they had managed to overpower my entire tribe. Maybe, with Bastien's help, I'd stand a better chance.

I wasn't sure what else to do other than lift back in the air and hurtle in the opposite direction, once again toward the ocean.

It seems I will have to take this into my own hands after all…

GRACE

When I woke up after the long rest Corrine insisted I take, I was still aching all over. My nose, especially. It had been mangled by the transformation and I suspected that I would have to wear a bandage over it for a while to come. Corrine said she could attempt to use her magic on it, but it was best to let it heal by itself.

I sat up, rubbing my eyes before inspecting the rest of my body. Corrine had wrapped up the tips of my fingers and toes with bandages, so that I didn't have to get freaked out every time I looked down and saw my nails missing. She had assured me that they would grow back fine, they just needed time. The same went for my missing hair. Though I was holding out hope that the jinn might be able to make that grow back more quickly.

But whatever the case, the state of my body could hardly get me down right now. I was just so relieved to finally be back. Ever since I'd been bitten by the Bloodless, I'd spent each minute either living in fear that I would turn, or experiencing the terror of being trapped as a Bloodless. Even now, I found my mind returning to that fearful state because it was so engrained in my consciousness.

I breathed in deeply. *I'm fine now. I'm safe. And so is Lawrence.*

I was brimming with excitement to see him again. We had been apart for so long it would feel like rediscovering one another.

I slid my legs off the bed and stood up—at least, I tried to stand up. I felt too weak, in spite of the bowl of broth Corrine had forced me to eat before I fell asleep.

Then I noticed that somebody had thoughtfully left a wheelchair at the end of my bed. Corrine probably left it in case I woke up and needed to use the bathroom by myself.

I lowered myself into the wheelchair and rolled myself to the bathroom. I stopped in front of the sink. Gripping hold of its edge, I pulled myself upward, keeping myself propped against it while I brushed my teeth and washed my face. At least my teeth had become normal again—for the most part. They seemed to be slightly sharper at the tips than I remembered them being, unless that was my imagination.

I sank back down into the chair, wheeled myself through the bedroom, and then into the hallway outside.

The sight of my father and Lawrence talking on a bench brought a smile to my face. They soon noticed me as I rolled toward them, their expressions mirroring mine.

"How are you feeling?" my father asked.

"Weak," I said, realizing how husky my voice was. "And achy. But I'm okay. I'll pull through."

He bent down to hug me and kiss my cheek.

"Where is Mom?" I asked him.

"She'll, uh, be here soon."

My eyes turned to Lawrence.

My father took the hint and said, "I'll give you two some time alone."

He resumed his seat on the bench, even as Lawrence moved around me and began to push my wheelchair into my room.

He pushed me right to the bed before leaning down and helping me out of it, propping me on the edge of the mattress.

I couldn't control the grin on my face as he sat down next to me.

"This is… surreal," Lawrence said, voicing my thoughts exactly.

"Yeah," I murmured. Now that I thought of it, I was pretty sure that this was the same room that Lawrence had been brought to initially, when he had first arrived in The Shade. "Spooky."

"Things are a lot less spooky now than they were a few hours ago," Lawrence muttered.

I let out a dry laugh, before we both fell into silence. Things turned unexpectedly awkward between us as we gazed into each other's eyes.

Then we both spoke at once:

"Grace, I—"

"Lawrence—"

We stopped at the same time, laughing.

I drew in a breath. "Lawrence… Just kiss me, will you?"

He was more than happy to oblige.

His arms moved around me and he drew me to him, placing my legs over his lap so that our faces could reach each other comfortably. Our lips inches apart, he closed his eyes and leaned closer, catching my lips in his. Exhilaration rushed through me. This wasn't our first kiss, but we were alone this time, and for that reason, it felt like the first time all over again. Sweet, tender, passionate. All-consuming. I laid my arms over his shoulders while his palms grazed the small of my back, pulling me closer still.

As we drew apart for a breath, he said, "You can stay sick for as long as you like, Grace. I owe you a few rides in that wheelchair."

I chuckled. "Thanks. Though I really don't intend to drag out my recovery if I can help it."

Truth be told, I was feeling very insecure right now. I was hardly looking my best—Miss Baldy with no nails. And here was Lawrence, looking—I wasn't going to mince my words—damn hot, as this new macho man he had become. It almost felt like I didn't deserve him.

I quickly pushed aside those thoughts, however, as he seemed to sense my self-consciousness. Maybe it was the way I had flinched as his fingertips brushed the base of my scalp, where my hair should've been.

His warm brown eyes gazed deep into mine as his thumbs caressed my cheeks. "You will always be beautiful to me, Grace," he said, his voice soft and husky. "Always."

I supposed he hadn't exactly looked his best when he first arrived in The Shade.

As he moved in to kiss me again, I couldn't help but grip his chin, stalling him and asking with one brow raised, "Even when I was a Bloodless?"

A smirk peeled across his face. "Uh, that's probably pushing it a bit…"

I snorted as I let go of his chin and allowed him to reclaim my lips.

We leaned backward on the bed, rolling onto our sides and facing each other as we continued to lose ourselves in each other.

We were interrupted by an abrupt knock at the door. It burst wide open a second later. I barely managed to sit up before Orlando stepped into the room.

His face had been filled with anticipation, excitement—no doubt he had just heard that I had woken up, and he'd come in to greet me—but now he froze in his tracks. His face fell as he gazed at me, still wrapped in Lawrence's arms.

"Orlando," I managed, wiping my mouth with the back of my hand. "Hey, how are you?"

His eyes returned fleetingly to me from Lawrence before he replied vaguely, "I'm fine… Just came in to see how you were. No worries. I'll check back another time."

He turned swiftly to leave the room.

"Wait," I called, attempting to stand but remembering my weakness.

Orlando paused by the door, glancing furtively at me.

"The antidote," I said. "When are we going to try it on you?"

"In a bit," he said. "Corrine's going to take me into her spell room with Dr. Finnegan so the two of them can examine my blood before giving me a dose… there's just enough ingredients left in those tubes for me, or so they said."

"I want to know how it goes," I told him.

Orlando smiled fleetingly. "I'm sure you'll hear from me about it, or through the grapevine." With that, he left the room.

As Lawrence pulled me back down next to him and kissed me again, I felt a horrible twinge of guilt. *Poor Orlando.* He had been so good to me… I didn't know how to respond to the longing in his eyes. I didn't feel for him what I felt for Lawrence. We didn't share the same spark. I loved Orlando but in a different way. Unfortunately for him, it looked like he was going to find himself trapped in the biggest cliché of all time. *"I love you as my friend, Orlando,"* I imagined myself saying. *Ugh. Lame.* But it was the truth. I wasn't sure what else to be with Orlando but honest.

I needed to catch up with him. I owed him a heart to heart—and more.

But for now, I continued enjoying my time with Lawrence, whom I could now safely call my boyfriend.

* * *

Lawrence and I were left alone for about another half

hour, before a second knock came at the door.

This time, it was my parents. They didn't burst in as quickly as Orlando had, so Lawrence and I had more time to sit up and compose ourselves before they entered. To my surprise, my mother's eyes were shining with tears.

"Mom? What's wrong?" I asked her. Yet as she approached, I wasn't sure if that was really the right question. Though she was crying, she did not look exactly sad. She just looked… breathlessly emotional.

She knelt down on the floor before me and held my hands. She kissed each of them before her turquoise eyes fixed on mine.

"You have a brother, Grace. A long-lost brother."

RIVER

As soon as I had laid eyes on Field, one of the Hawk half-blood boys, something stirred within me. It was his eyes. Aquamarine eyes, so close a shade to my own.

But as soon as they had arrived, everything became a blur of excitement and urgency. We were sure that we had the final ingredient to cure Grace. We had immediately gone about preparing the antidote and feeding it to Grace—but all the while, I kept glancing at Field. When he had offered to give his blood, I could hardly control my emotions. I was so sure that this was some twist of providence—my unknown and long-lost child returned to save his sibling.

After Corrine ushered everybody out of Grace's room so

that she could sleep, all I wanted to do was verify for a fact whether my instincts were accurate. I hadn't wanted to unsettle Field—so I didn't start stalking him or even talking to him. I waited with Ben in the hallway outside Grace's room until Corrine emerged.

"I need you to carry out a DNA test," I had told her.

She seemed to already be thinking along the same lines as me. She didn't even ask whose blood I wanted to test—she already knew it was Field.

Ben, Corrine and I headed to the Sanctuary. Corrine already had a sample of Grace's blood from prior to Grace's turning, when she'd been trying to figure out how to stop the impending transformation. Grace's blood would make for a better sample than my vampire blood.

Corrine wanted her spell room to herself as she started work, so Ben and I waited outside.

It was a bizarre feeling to be sitting there, waiting for Corrine's news. I could hardly express it. I wasn't sure what my reaction would be if it came up positive. I shared a son with somebody I didn't even know. It must have been just as strange and uncomfortable for Ben. I held his gaze, wondering what he was thinking. He placed a hand on my knee and squeezed it, even as he kissed my cheek. He looked deep into my eyes and held the side of my face.

"Whatever the result turns out to be," he said gently,

"don't think that it will change anything… If Field is your son, then he will be mine, too."

Tears welled in my eyes as I clutched Ben's face and kissed him hard. "I love you, Ben," I whispered.

He held me close, providing me comfort when I needed it most. Anchoring me when I felt adrift in uncertainty.

We were hardly breathing as Corrine finally emerged. It was hard to tell the result from her expression alone. She was doing a good job at pulling a poker face as she made her way toward us. The wait only made me more tense.

She ran her tongue over her lower lip before glancing from Ben to me. "Well," she said, "would you really like to know the answer?"

Ugh. "Yes!" Ben and I urged at once.

"Okay… Your instincts were correct. Field is your son."

Although I had truthfully been expecting this answer all along, I still wasn't quite prepared for the tsunami of emotions that came over me. I wasn't sure what to feel: excitement, that Grace had a sibling she'd so often said she'd wished for; grief, on considering what a terrible, neglected life Field had lived in my absence; or fear, over how this was all going to work. And over everything, curiosity burned within me to know who his father was. Whether he was even still alive.

My emotions manifested in uncontrollable tears. I found

myself shaking and sobbing in Ben's arms, even as he held me firmly and kissed my temple.

"Hey, it's okay, baby," he whispered, rubbing my back. "It's okay."

Could I even be a mother to him? Would he even accept me? Would he accept Ben?

We were complete strangers to each other. I wondered if the bridge between us could ever be closed.

This was all so strange. Stranger than a dream.

Corrine gave Ben and me some privacy, and I continued to cry in his arms until I could cry no more. I drew in deep shuddering breaths as I tried to compose myself. *I should listen to what my husband said. It's okay. It's going to be okay.*

"We can go and talk to him in your own time," Ben said. "There's no rush."

I nodded, clearing my throat. Though I actually did not want to drag this out. I wanted to talk to Field, now. Drawing it out would only leave me to speculate longer about how it would all go. How it would all work out.

I clutched Ben's hand and kissed the back of it before raising my eyes to his. "I'd like to talk to him now. And I think that, at least initially, I should see him alone."

* * *

Corrine escorted us back to the hospital. We found the

five boys on the ground floor, sitting around a table in the dining room. They were gulping down a meal. Who knew the last time they had eaten proper food. Maybe even never.

I stood with Ben discreetly in the doorway of the dining hall, waiting until they had finished before daring to venture in alone and make my way toward Field, while Ben headed up to Grace's room. Field was just dumping his disposable plate into a trashcan and I caught him turning around, our turquoise eyes meeting. He stopped still as he stared back at me, his thick brows lowering. Now that I examined him, I was sure that we shared a similar lip shape, too.

My voice caught in my throat. "Field," I managed. "Could I... have a word with you?"

He looked at me uncertainly, but nodded. I sat down at an empty table with him, the two of us in opposite seats. I hesitated. *How do I break this to him?* I guessed there was really only one way... "Field, I... I'm your mother."

He looked like he'd been stunned. His lips parting, his breath hitched. "What?"

"You were born from my egg. You are my son."

God, this felt so weird. I could only imagine how Grace would react once I told her.

"One of our witches did a test," I went on, my voice

becoming more unsteady.

"*Mother?*" he mouthed.

"I'm afraid I don't know who your father is," I said. *So don't ask me that.* Although I was curious, there was a part of me that hoped I would never find out who his father was. It would take the strangeness of the situation to a whole new level.

Field's face only grew more stunned as I went on to explain how he must have been conceived. How my eggs had been stolen, and I never knew about his existence. How I never would have known, had it not been for Lawrence finding and bringing him here.

I talked and talked, and by the end, when he was still silent, I couldn't bear to sit here facing him any longer. I stood up and moved around to him, placing my hands on his shoulders. He rose and, even as he stood much taller than me, I drew him in for a hug.

He was stiff at first beneath my embrace, but then his arms loosened and wrapped around me. These boys weren't used to affection. I doubted Field had ever been hugged. The only constant in their lives had been each other.

I couldn't stop the tears leaking from my eyes again now, even though I wished that they wouldn't.

As we drew apart, my hands running down his arms and clasping his hands, we looked each other over again.

"Mother," he repeated, as though he still couldn't believe it. Neither could I. It would take a while for this revelation to sink in for all of us.

As I turned, I realized the other four boys were watching us. Unfortunately, I had no idea who their parents were. I couldn't spot any of my traits in them, so I could only assume it was just Field created from one of my eggs. I wasn't sure that my nerves could have hacked two surprise sons, so it was just as well.

"I'd like to take you to your half-sister," I told Field. "She doesn't know about our connection yet. Would you mind that?"

"I'd like it."

"Okay," I breathed.

Still holding Field's hand, I led him out of the room and to the elevators, where we ascended to Grace's floor. As we emerged and I caught sight of Ben, a warm smile spread across his face.

I led Field to him and introduced Ben. "This is my husband," I told him. I was tempted to add, *And the closest thing you have to a father,* but there would be time for that later.

Field was in too much of a daze to smile back at Ben.

"And Grace, whom your blood saved, is your sibling," I continued. "Is Grace awake?" I asked Ben.

"Yes. She came out here just a short while ago. Lawrence is with her now."

I turned to Field. "Let me go in and break the news to her. Then you can meet her a second, proper time."

Ben and I left Field in the hallway and entered Grace's room to find her and Lawrence sitting on the bed. As I hurried to my daughter and knelt before her, I told her everything about Corrine's findings. Her expression mirrored Field's uncannily.

"Oh, my God," she said, her voice choking up. "Wh- Where is he?"

I took that as my cue to return to the corridor and bring Field in. He eyed Grace nervously, then slowly moved toward her. As Grace attempted to stand up, Lawrence assisted her, holding her waist and steadying her as she reached out to brush her hand against Field's right arm.

Through her moistening eyes, a smile shone through.

"My brother," she managed, before throwing her arms around him and holding him in a tight hug. Then I heard her whisper into his ear: "Thank you."

GRACE

My brother.

I had a brother. I had heard my mother's words and yet I still couldn't believe it. Even in spite of his eyes, so close a color to my own. He had my mother's lips, too.

Field's expression was that of confusion, uncertainty, as though we both shared the same doubts. Could this really be happening?

"Are you sure, Mom?" I couldn't help but clarify, even though I knew she would never have told me if she was not completely certain.

"Corrine ran a DNA test," she said, her voice deep. "It's true."

This was so weird. Who was—*or is*—Field's father? This must have been even weirder for my dad.

My mother explained to me in brief the gaps in my knowledge about Field's appearance in The Shade—how and where Lawrence had found him and the other four young men. After that, none of us really knew what to say for a while. We just sat in the room and looked at each other.

"So you've basically lived your life alone, with your other four… brothers?" Even though they weren't related—or at least, didn't appear to be—'brother' seemed to be the right term to use.

"Yes," he replied.

"Since you escaped the harpies and left the supernatural dimension, you've been in Canada… in that cave, all those years?"

"Yes," he said again.

His tone was stiff. Considering that he had just discovered his long-lost family, I would've thought he'd look more emotional. But it seemed that he'd never really been in an environment to develop emotionally. Harpies had been the closest thing he'd had to parents.

I felt almost guilty. My life had been so easy, so carefree and happy, compared to his.

I felt the urge to understand him more. I wished to know him. But I found myself faltering, uncertain of even what questions to ask next. It felt like we were from two totally different worlds. I didn't know how to relate to him. All the usual questions I would've asked a stranger—about hobbies, favorite subjects, and so on—didn't seem to be applicable here. His life appeared to have been just one long, hard struggle, from his birth, up until now—all a fight for survival. But I knew there were deeper levels to him, just as there were to all of us. I supposed it would be a slow process, a matter of time and patience as he settled into our environment in The Shade.

All I could think to do now was hold his hands, pull him in and hug him again tightly. Then I kissed his cool, pale cheek.

"Do you know when your birthday is?" I asked, I wanted to know whether he was older or younger than me. He looked like he could be older, but that could simply be his mature demeanor.

He shook his head. "I don't know—"

There came a knock at the door. My mother called, "Come in!" and in stepped Field's four companions. They gave no explanation for their entrance. They simply entered and stood behind Field, looking around the room, before their eyes settled on my mother and me. I looked at them curiously, from their scruffy clothing to their long, untamed hair.

The fact that they felt no need to give an explanation for their interruption of what would look to most people like a private conversation made me realize that they simply weren't used to being apart. It was normal for them to do everything together. Be everywhere together. And they didn't expect anybody to think that was odd.

"Why don't you take a seat?" my mother said with a warm smile. She pulled up chairs for each of them, and they sat down around us.

"Well," my mother said, looking back at Field, "maybe we'll have to decide on a birthday for you."

We sat with each other a while longer—the other boys were a little more talkative than Field, asking questions about our island and how it came to be. Then my mother suggested that she go and find them some spare accommodations where they could have a shower, and be provided with some new clothes… as well as a haircut, if they wanted it. None of them volunteered for the latter, though they were all accepting of accommodations and clothing.

I remained staring at Field as he stood up, and all of them headed out of the room with my mother.

Field reminded me of somebody who had been traumatized—out of touch with other people and himself. He had a lot of growing to do emotionally. But I found myself looking forward to spending more time with him. To cracking him, chiseling away at his stony exterior and discovering the young man he really was underneath. *My brother.*

I felt in a daze as the door shut behind them. I even forgot momentarily that Lawrence was still with me in the room.

I turned to look at Lawrence, my eyes widening. "Just when you think life can't get any stranger," I murmured.

He chuckled. "I know the feeling."

I lay back on the bed, heaving out a long, deep sigh and staring up at the ceiling. "At least *you're* not my long-lost sibling."

"Consider me glad, too," Lawrence muttered.

"You could have been, for all I knew, when we found you in the basement in The Woodlands... You could have been some genetic experiment. You even showed symptoms of a half-blood."

"I was closer to a Bloodless than I ever was to a vampire," Lawrence said. "I still am, though you wouldn't know it by looking at me."

I sat up abruptly as I remembered Orlando. "Oh! Let's go and check on Orlando. He's supposed to be taking the antidote—probably anytime now."

Lawrence stole a kiss from me before sitting me upright and helping me into my wheelchair. Then he pushed me out of the room and into the hallway outside.

"Where is Orlando supposed to be?" he asked, as we glanced up and down.

"Let's head down that way," I said, pointing to our left. There weren't many doors to our right, and all of them appeared to be open.

As we moved along, Lawrence briefly pressed an ear against each closed door until he stopped, about seven along. "Sounds like Corrine is in here."

He pushed me to the door and allowed me to listen too. It was Corrine. I reached out and knocked.

We entered to find Orlando lying in bed, Corrine by his side.

"Hey," I said, offering him a smile as Lawrence pushed me toward them. "What's going on?"

"We gave Orlando the antidote," Corrine said, eyeing him. "He seems to be making progress. Of course, the change is not going to be as drastic as it was with you. But if the antidote can purge the Bloodless virus from Orlando's system, which is what is making him so ill, he should be healthy again very soon."

I narrowed my eyes, examining his complexion. I didn't think it was my imagination—he definitely looked warmer than the last time I saw him… Though that had been just when he had walked in on me and Lawrence kissing. I could hardly expect him not to have a pale face after witnessing that.

"How are you feeling?" I asked Orlando.

He avoided my gaze. "Fine."

"I've got to go and check on some things," Corrine said, patting Orlando on the arm. "You stay here and rest."

As Corrine left, I glanced at Lawrence. I really owed Orlando some time, just the two of us. "Hey, Lawrence, do you mind giving Orlando and me a few minutes?"

"Sure," Lawrence said, even as he frowned slightly. "I'll, uh, wait outside."

He backed out of the room and closed the door politely behind him, while I returned my focus to Orlando. Now that we were on our own, he looked at me. His brown eyes were glassy.

I reached out and held his hand, which felt almost warm. "Hey. I... I wanted to talk about earlier." *About us.* "Lawrence... he's my boyfriend."

Orlando nodded, curtly. "Oh, I know. I saw."

My lips felt a tad dry all of a sudden. "I'm sorry."

Orlando shook his head, while his eyes wandered to the other side of the room. "Nothing to apologize for."

I hated how abrupt he was being. How cold and distant. How shut off.

But I wasn't sure what more to say. He clearly didn't want to be having this conversation. So I merely swallowed, squeezed his hand and said, "I guess I'll leave you to rest now... I'm so relieved the procedure went okay. You really do look like you're recovering."

"Yeah," he said faintly.

I gripped the wheels of my chair and backed myself away from his bed. After casting one last, guilt-ridden look over at Orlando, who was still determinedly avoiding me, I headed to the door and rolled outside. Lawrence was waiting for me on a bench in the hallway.

He gave me a questioning look as I approached, but he did not ask me anything. He waited for me to offer an answer, which I gave after we had moved back down the hallway and into my room.

Lawrence sat on the edge of the bed while I stayed in my chair. I took his hand in mine and rested it on my lap while gazing down at it.

"Some time ago, Orlando kissed me," I said quietly.

Lawrence went still, though he swallowed rather audibly.

"He did it just a few hours before I found you in Aviary."
A few hours before I kissed you.

I raised Lawrence's hand and placed a kiss over the back of it, finally meeting his gaze. I didn't like how uncomfortable he looked. "I love you, Lawrence," I said softly. "And I told Orlando that you're my boyfriend. I just... I worry for him."

I wouldn't even be alive if it wasn't for Orlando. Although Maura had also helped in saving me from the Bloodless down in that sewage tunnel in Bloodless Chicago, it had been Orlando who had convinced her to allow me to come with them. I wouldn't have lasted another hour if they hadn't taken me up to that rooftop hideout.

Lawrence breathed in. "Well… I, uh… I'm not sure what to say."

"I don't expect you to say anything. I just needed to tell you."

Lawrence nodded. "I understand."

I leaned in to kiss the side of Lawrence's face, my lips grazing his stubble. He wrapped his arms around me.

I just hoped that Orlando was going to be okay. Even if he was cured now, and was no longer waiting to die, he struck me as quite the tightly strung sort. Without his sister… and now without me… I couldn't *help* but worry for him.

VICTORIA

We could only speculate about what had happened to Yuraya. But Bastien feared that she might have returned to The Woodlands to report us to the Mortclaws.

I was not sure what we could do. How could we run? The Mortclaws could locate us with their supernatural senses.

If they were indeed coming after us, they would hunt us down faster than the three of us could make it back to The Woodlands to seek Mona's help. I tried carrying both Bastien and Cecil at once, but I traveled far slower and it was tiring. I wasn't a full Mortclaw, after all. I was still primarily human, and my newfound strength only stretched so far.

It seemed incredibly dangerous to begin our journey

across the ocean—for who knew how many miles—when I wasn't sure I would even have the strength to complete it with their extra weight pulling me down. If we found ourselves stranded, we would be without a boat, and at risk from all kinds of dangerous water beasts.

It seemed that our only option was to stay put and make our way back to The Woodlands as fast as we could travel by vessel. If we met the Mortclaws on the way, then… so be it.

Bastien, of course, pushed for me to fly away alone, back to Mona. But I reminded him in a rather terse manner that I was his wife now, and I had chosen to stay.

I feared that Bastien was at risk from them, even though he was Sendira's son. Those Mortclaws were so unpredictable. I would not put anything past them.

And so, with tense chests, we went on with our journey.

We stayed close to each other on the deck, huddled together in the control cabin with Cecil. If Bastien's family did arrive, we would be better off together than scattered around different parts of the ship.

I began to mistake every flock of birds in the sky for the Mortclaws zooming in our direction.

Finally, I spotted the harrowing sight I had been waiting for… well, not exactly.

It was a single werewolf hurtling toward us.

Bastien immediately shot to his feet, gripping my arm and

pushing me behind him. Which I found rather ironic. Of the two of us, I was actually more capable of defending myself from this young woman than Bastien was. I possessed supernatural speed and flight.

Within a few seconds, she had landed on the deck. She stood before us in her humanoid form.

Fury burned in her irises as they locked with Bastien's. I feared that she was about to shoot her laser-like fire... but she saved that for me.

As she turned to me, I saw what was coming before she could act. I hurtled into the air, and as I glanced back to check her distance, Yuraya looked stunned. She had not been expecting that. At all.

Maybe I took a page or two out of your book, wolf.

Recovering, she zoomed after me with renewed vigor. As she chased after me in the sky, I refused to look back in case I met her eyes. But I could sense that she was closing in on me far faster than was comfortable.

In an attempt to shake her off at least somewhat, I dove into the water and passed beneath the boat. I burst out on the other side.

That hardly did much to distract her. She was already catching up again.

As fast as I could travel, I exchanged a panicked glance with Bastien. I didn't know how to handle the situation.

Keep running from her? She would only keep chasing me until she had me in her grip, turned into a wolf and tore me apart—likely eating me in the process.

Even if I was supposedly one of her own, any connection she might have felt to me because of the potion was completely overpowered by her sheer envy. I could have been her sister and she would have acted the same.

"Yuraya!" Bastien bellowed up. I could see how frustrated he was, being bound to the ground. If he could fly, he would have been chasing after her. "Come down here!" he demanded of her. "Talk to me!" ·

I would have let out a dry chuckle had I not been so focused on dodging Yuraya as she lunged for me. Talking was obviously the last thing that Yuraya planned on doing for a while.

"Leave her alone!" he roared. "If you want to fight, do it with someone your own size. Come and fight me!"

What was Bastien saying? He wasn't *her own size*. He wasn't anywhere near her size once she had transformed into a wolf. She was a giant.

To my horror, Yuraya paused in the sky and glanced down at Bastien.

I couldn't believe that she was actually considering his words and averting her focus from me.

"And what if I won, Bastien? What if I pinned you down

and squashed your throat until you were one breath away from your last? Then what? What difference would it make?" Her voice faltered and, to my surprise, the corners of her eyes moistened. "You would still not love me! You have given yourself to this… this bitch!"

"Come down here," Bastien repeated, his voice remarkably steady. "Come down here to my level."

As I distanced myself from her, she glanced up at me, reluctance filling her face. I was just about ready to avert my eyes again in case she shot more fire, but then, with a shuddering sigh, she descended to the deck in front of Bastien. Now I found myself lowering, afraid of what she was going to do next. I could hardly imagine a more unpredictable creature than a slighted she-wolf. They could be hard to predict even at the best of times.

Bastien eyed her with similar trepidation. He took a step back, maintaining his distance from her like she was an escaped zoo animal. Which, really, she was.

"You are my cousin," Bastien said, looking her firmly in the eye. "You and I will always have a connection because of that. We are family. Your blood runs in mine… But I do not love you as my wife. I do not love you in that way, and I could not make you happy if we were married. I would leave you unfulfilled. Because you could never fulfill me. Victoria is my mate now. We have bonded. You need to accept that."

Ouch.

Bastien was trying to be honest with her, but oh, dear, I did not see that going well.

It didn't.

She immediately started seething again, and in a burst of fury, she leapt on Bastien and began ripping apart his clothes.

He wrestled with her, trying to get her under control, but her strength was too much for him. Panicking, I lowered to the deck, looking for anything that I could use to pry her off.

"Victoria!" Cecil hissed.

Having been backed up against a corner in fear, now he fumbled against his belt and drew out a small dagger. He shoved it into my hands.

I stared at the blade glinting in my hands, but only for three seconds.

There was no asking a wolf like Yuraya. With the sound of Bastien's struggles loud in my ears, there was only one thing that I could think to do.

Tightening my grip around the knife, I surged forward. Her back was still facing me as she maintained control over Bastien. I rose into the air behind her. My heart thumping, I lifted the blade and brought it down, plunging it into the back of her neck.

She let out a frightening choking sound, her grip around Bastien loosening. Her arms rose behind her, hands clutching at the blade. They closed around the hilt and managed to pull it out… but the damage had been done. She coughed and spluttered, blood beginning to spill from her lips.

I stared at her, hardly believing what I had just done.

Even if, as a Mortclaw, she possessed healing powers, I doubted they would be strong enough to get her out of this. I had fatally wounded her.

Everything seemed to happen in slow motion—her knees giving way, her crumpling flat on the ground, her blood pooling around her.

Cecil, Bastien and I stood stunned.

Oh, my. What have I done?

MONA

What were we going to do? The question still plagued Brock and me as we held the Mortclaws hostage outside Blackhall Mountain.

Brock suggested that maybe we ought to get rid of them, kill them, since they were only going to continue killing others in our absence. But that didn't sit right with me. These days, I did everything I possibly could to avoid claiming another's life.

They were Bastien's parents and pack, after all. Victoria's parents-in-law if they ever got married. They ought to be treated with some respect at least, for that reason alone.

I had already exchanged strong words with them,

informing the werewolves—as if they didn't know—that it was simply not appropriate to eat their fellow citizens, and that I would not stand for it. But they had replied with what I knew all along: that they couldn't help but crave their fellow wolves' flesh. They had been touched by the black witches—whom I had assisted at the time—and that was what gave them their craving.

I sat down on the grass, mulling over our options even as my eyes remained on the line of giant werewolves.

Somehow, we needed to remove this ghastly spell from them. I pulled out the vial from my bag and gazed at it. Those black witches, even after their death, had left behind a legacy of destruction.

I could only be thankful that Rhys had made his exit from the world when he had.

I sloshed the liquid around and around in the glass. Breaking this vial would put a stop to their cannibalism for sure. But the problem was, I did not know exactly what else it might put a stop to. It could potentially put their very lives in the balance, which meant that even Bastien and Victoria could be affected, both of whom had consumed the elixir to differing degrees.

"What are you thinking?" my son asked, slumping down next to me.

"I'm thinking that we need to find a way to lift the spell.

Transform them back into regular wolves, the way they were before Rhys came along and meddled with them."

They might've been a strong tribe to begin with, but they were still werewolves, like the others. Even if they retained their craving for cannibalism, for their fellow wolves' flesh, at least they would no longer have such an unfair advantage. The other wolf packs could conceivably band together to protect themselves. As it was, the Mortclaws were simply killing machines. There was no fight involved. The Mortclaws decided who they wanted to attack and eat, and it was done.

The black witches had meddled with nature's balance in The Woodlands by creating these abominations, and somehow, we had to put it back.

"What if you opened the vial and tried to… I don't know, *alter* the potion somehow?" Brock suggested.

I frowned doubtfully. "I could try it," I said. "But again, I'm worried about Bastien and Victoria."

"But whatever you did wouldn't be as harmful as smashing the vial, would it? The risk wouldn't be so great?" Brock pressed.

He had a point. "No. If I was cautious, the risk should not be as great."

"Then maybe some risks have to be taken," Brock said.

The other option, of course, was to attempt to lock the

Mortclaws away again. But what if at some point in the future, they somehow found a way back out again? I did not like unfinished business, and simply bundling these creatures back in a hole felt like just that. It felt like we needed to solve this problem, once and for all.

I heaved a sigh and wandered back over to the Mortclaws, holding their gazes as I walked past each of them.

"Can you *really* not control your appetite?" I asked, my eyes narrowing on them. "Or is this cannibalism just a form of greed?"

They were too angry to speak with me anymore. They merely growled and yelled at me to let them free.

Well, if you won't answer the questions, perhaps we'll have to attempt to find out by ourselves…

Victoria

It took five minutes for the reality to sink in. Yuraya was gone, and she was not coming back.

I handed Bastien an old blanket I found on the deck, which he fashioned to cover himself, then helped him to his feet.

Bastien swallowed hard. "Well," he said. "We can't just leave her here."

"What do you suggest we do?" I asked.

Bastien looked at Cecil. The old man didn't look like he had any ideas.

"Should we slip her body into the ocean?" I asked.

Bastien bit his lip. I guessed from his hesitation that this was not done in werewolf tradition; it must be important to families to give their departed a proper funeral ceremony.

I shuddered to think about what would happen once the rest of the Mortclaws found out. As if they didn't already have enough reason to hate me, now I had gone and murdered the woman they had picked out as Bastien's betrothed since his birth. I still didn't understand how Yuraya knew that Bastien was to be her betrothed. From what I understood, it was supposed to be the groom who broke the news to the bride. Maybe Sendira had deemed that particular tradition as breakable, in order to put more pressure on her son. Whatever the case, it was irrelevant now.

Silently, Bastien bent down and scooped her body up from the deck, leaving a trail of blood behind him. He raised her over the edge of the ship and dropped her into the waves.

"We have no choice," he said hoarsely.

We stood and stared at the area where Yuraya had sunk, our nerves still recovering.

Then Cecil asked nervously, "So what now?"

My mind turned to Mona and Brock, waiting for me in The Woodlands. I hated to think how long I had kept them hanging around already. I really needed to get back to them.

But getting back to them meant returning to the Mortclaws.

We still weren't sure why Yuraya had returned to the ship

without them, but I could only guess that she had not managed to tell them yet about Bastien and me. Which meant that our trip back to The Woodlands should in theory be safer than we'd thought it would be only less than an hour ago. I wasn't sure if the Mortclaws could sense when one of their kind had passed away, the same way they could sense location. I hadn't felt anything, though I had only been influenced by a small amount of the elixir.

"We should return," Bastien said firmly after another pause. His expression was ashen, but resigned. "We can't keep running away forever. We have to return to the witches, and we have to solve this problem once and for all."

We didn't talk much on the journey back to The Woodlands. I grew tenser with each hour that passed until finally the familiar outline of the Woodlands came into view in the distance.

We left the ship and arrived on the land, gazing around cautiously.

"I think we should head straight to Blackhall Mountain," I said. "That's where I left Mona and Brock. They said that they would hang around and wait for me there."

Bastien nodded. "We need to return Cecil too."

And so we set off through The Woodlands, each of us

running at supernatural speed. Cecil appeared tired, but even at his old age his speed was nothing to scoff at—at least, compared to a human's.

The closer we got to Blackhall Mountain, disconcertingly, the more I sensed the Mortclaws' presence. Bastien seemed to sense them too. His gray eyes shone with anxiety. All of us feared the worst as we forged onward until we arrived in the clearing outside the Blackhalls' lair.

I was expecting to see a bloody massacre, and while the ground appeared to be stained with blood, there were no fallen Blackhalls that I could see. Just the Mortclaws, all lined up in a row on the edge of the forest, Mona and Brock in front of them.

I gasped in relief. "Oh, thank God." They had gotten the Mortclaws under control already. I couldn't have imagined a more relieving sight than the monsters frozen on the ground as we made our way toward them. Maybe, finally, luck was on our side.

On hearing our approach, Mona and Brock turned around. Their eyes widened as they spotted us.

"You did it!" Mona exclaimed, looking quite disbelieving. "You found him!"

"Yes," I said, my eyes falling once again on the Mortclaws. "And... look what you did..."

"Bastien!" Sendira shrilled out. She was slumped against

the base of a tree. "Son, you must help free us!"

Bastien's gaze moved fleetingly to his mother, and then to his father, who called out a similar plea. But then his focus returned to the bloodstained ground behind us. His face went pale. "What happened here?" he asked in a hushed tone, as though he feared the answer.

Mona's expression saddened. "We found the Mortclaws attacking Blackhall Mountain. We managed to arrive toward the beginning of the attack, and prevented excessive damage, but some werewolves lost their lives. I'm sorry, Bastien."

Oh, no.

"The Blackhalls were supposed to have evacuated!" Bastien looked wounded. "They must have decided to stay and defend our territory… Who died?"

"I don't know," Mona said, shrugging, "but they headed back into the mountain."

Bastien immediately turned on his heel and rushed toward the mountain, Cecil on his heels, while I remained with Mona and Brock.

"How long have you been keeping them here like this?" I asked.

"Several hours," Mona replied. "I've kind of lost track."

"What happened with you?" Brock asked, eyeing me, his brows raised.

I looked nervously at the Mortclaws. I didn't want to talk

to Mona and Brock about everything that had happened within the wolves' earshot, so the witches would have to wait.

"Release us!" Sendira roared out.

Training my eyes on her, I moved toward her and stopped a few feet away. Blood still stained the corners of her mouth.

Given that she was now my mother-in-law, it felt almost wrong, disrespectful to be looming over her as I was, but I couldn't help but remind her, "This is all your own doing, Sendira. If you insist on terrorizing other wolves and eating their flesh, you cannot be allowed to continue roaming The Woodlands freely. This is the price you pay for not controlling your appetite."

Sendira snarled.

I wouldn't tell her yet that Bastien and I had married. I would leave it to Bastien to break that particular piece of news to her.

I waited awkwardly with Mona and Brock until Bastien returned to us from the mountain.

He now looked grief-stricken.

"What happened?" I asked.

"They've already held a funeral for the dead," he croaked. "Four lives were lost."

I hugged him tight, hoping to instill in him some comfort.

Sendira really did not like that.

"How dare you touch my son!"

Bastien's grief bled into anger as his eyes rose to his parents and other family members. Leaving my side, he stalked toward them and glared.

I was surprised when he immediately came out with, "As you have just claimed four of my family, so I have claimed one of yours. Yuraya is dead. I killed her."

Gasps swept along the line of werewolves. I spotted a woman who looked like Yuraya, her mouth agape.

There was no regret in Bastien's eyes. He almost seemed to enjoy relaying the news. It seemed that he had finally snapped.

He reached back to grab me. I had approached him as he'd been addressing his family.

"Victoria is my mate now," he announced, "and if I hear one word of insult or protest against her, I will be sure to persuade these witches to lock you back up in the dungeon from whence you came for the rest of your miserable lives."

Bastien's chest was heaving as he turned his back on his stunned family, and looked firmly at Mona. "Please take us somewhere we can talk in private, without these cannibals."

Bastien

The grief of losing four members of my tribe caused my emotions to erupt. The Blackhall tribe had suffered enough with the recent loss of my foster family and then the worry of my and Cecil's abrupt disappearance. The last thing they needed was more upheaval.

At the sight of those Mortclaws frozen by the witches' spell, I couldn't stop myself from telling them exactly how I felt, be they my blood relatives or not.

Mona transported us to the other side of the woods that bordered the Blackhalls' clearing.

Now, once and for all, we had to find a solution for

dealing with these monsters. A permanent solution. Although I had threatened to have the Mortclaws imprisoned again, somehow, that didn't feel like a proper resolution to me. What if some self-interested party like Brucella saw some reason to release them again in the future and found a way to do it? I didn't want such atrocities to ever be repeated again in The Woodlands.

It seemed that Mona shared my thoughts. "I've been trying to settle this matter for good," she said. She retrieved a vial of greenish-brown liquid from her bag and showed it to me. This was the first time I had ever laid eyes on it—this vial of elixir, the cause of all of my family's problems. I wondered what my life would be like if the black witches had never entered The Woodlands. If the Mortclaws had remained as regular werewolves, albeit a stronger breed. Sendira would've still been a tough nut to crack, but it would've been nothing like this.

As I took the vial from Mona and stared at it, I felt so tempted to drop it, watch it smash into pieces.

If Victoria had not consumed some of it, and let it alter her being, I might have even taken the risk and done it; if it was only my life and the rest of my family's lives at stake. If I'd really thought that it could solve this problem, I would've let the vial slip.

"So what are your ideas?" I asked the witches.

"I don't have anything solid," Mona said, rubbing her forehead. "But Brock came up with the idea that I try to alter the potion in my spell room. I would need to return to The Shade for that, however. I doubt that Brock's and my spell will be strong enough to keep these powerful beasts incapacitated while I'm in another dimension. Brock's only a half-warlock, after all. If I leave, they will go free again and cause God knows how much more disruption until I return."

"What if you brewed up a spell while you're here in The Woodlands?" Victoria suggested. "You could tell Brock what equipment or ingredients you think you need, and we could go back, fetch them and bring them here for you."

Mona sighed, then looked to her son. "I'm not sure what exactly is going to be required... so you're going to find yourselves bringing back an awful lot."

Victoria

As horrid as it was to return and discover that several of Bastien's tribe members had been murdered, finding the Mortclaws under the control of Mona couldn't help but fill me with optimism—optimism that I had not felt for a long time. After all of Bastien's and my troubles, maybe things were finally turning around. Maybe we had almost reached the elusive light at the end of the tunnel.

I hadn't gotten over murdering Yuraya. The thought that I had claimed another person's life was traumatizing. It didn't matter how evil she was or what she had been trying to do, I had still shed blood. It would probably take weeks for the act to fully sink in.

But for now, I allowed my mind to wander to a happier place. Bastien and I had been through hell and back. As we returned to The Shade with Brock, I allowed the excitement to bubble up within me. I could see my parents and family again. That was, in fact, the main reason I'd wanted Bastien and I to accompany Brock back to The Shade, because we weren't exactly of any use to Brock in his mother's spell room. We had no idea about ingredients or equipment. I'd just wanted to get a ride back with him—however brief—to check in on life back on our beautiful island.

So much must have happened since I left. We wouldn't have much time to catch up, since I doubted it would take Brock long to gather up everything he needed. Bastien and I would have to make the best use of the time we had.

As Brock manifested us outside The Shade, we were forced to yell for someone to let us in because Brock didn't have special permission to enter.

Ibrahim came to our rescue swiftly and, after an identity check, settled us all down on the forest ground.

"What has been going on with you?" he asked.

Brock was already vanishing himself to his mother's spell room—I had told him that I wanted to go with Bastien to see my parents and that once he was done gathering everything he needed he could collect us. "Everything's going okay," I said confidently. Perhaps a little too confidently. "But we don't have time to talk now. We've only dropped back here so that Brock can pick up some of his mom's equipment, and then we need to head back to The Woodlands. I'm sorry, but I promise we'll update everyone as soon as we can."

I caught Bastien's hand and we left Ibrahim frowning after us. I led him to the Residences, to my parents' treehouse. My heart was racing as we ascended in the elevator. It felt like an age since I had last seen my mom and dad.

Arriving on the veranda, I peered through the kitchen window—nobody was visible—before knocking on the door.

I had to knock a second time before footsteps sounded. It was my father who came to the door. His hair looked mussed and he wore pajamas. I'd probably just woken him up. But his eyes soon sharpened. "Vicky!" he gasped, relief rolling over his expression. He scooped me up in a hug before turning to face Bastien.

He didn't know that there was anything different about me yet.

As he let go of me, my mother came hurrying to the door. "Vicky!" she exclaimed. I threw myself into her arms. She held me tight and showered kisses down on my face.

"Mom," I managed, my throat feeling constricted.

"You found Bastien!" she said.

My parents turned their attention to the wolf. He bowed his head respectfully. Then they ushered us inside.

We took a seat on a sofa in the sitting area, while my mother asked if either of us was hungry or thirsty. We accepted something to drink but there was no time to eat.

"We have to return to The Woodlands," I said. "Mona is still there."

I proceeded to explain to them what had happened since I'd last seen them—everything except my marriage to Bastien.

They stared at me, dumbstruck. "'You drank more from that vial?" my father clarified.

"Yes, but look at me. I'm okay." I lifted myself in the air before them, demonstrating my power.

"Oh, my," my mother said faintly.

I figured it would take a long time for them to get used to this… And I hadn't even told them yet about the marriage.

I glanced at Bastien, and it was as though he had read my thoughts. He looked quite nervous all of a sudden—something I found quite endearing. I smiled, taking his hand in mine before looking from my father to my mother. "I've actually become a Mortclaw in more ways than one," I began, tentatively.

They frowned at me, and I almost felt bad for hitting

them with this along with everything else I had just revealed. They already looked close to breaking down after learning that I had morphed into this strange, new creature.

"What are you saying?" my mother dared ask.

I had no ring to show them. Instead my fingers twined with Bastien's before I brought his hand to rest on my lap.

A wide grin settled in on my face. "Bastien and I are officially a couple... More than just a couple. We're married."

"What?" both of my parents asked at once, staring at the two of us, disbelieving.

At this, Bastien cleared his throat and spoke for the first time. "I hope you will excuse me for taking the liberty of asking your daughter to be mine, even in your absence. But I love your daughter. And I promise that I will take care of her."

"You... you had a wedding?" my mother asked incredulously. "In The Woodlands?"

"No," I said. "We had a small ceremony on the boat as we were traveling back to The Woodlands from The Dunes. Cecil was there to witness it."

They both fell silent.

They looked not only sore, but also shocked that I'd gone forward with something like this without even a word to them. But what word could I have possibly gotten to them?

When Bastien had proposed to me back on the ship, I couldn't help but accept. Everything about that moment had felt right. The last thing I'd wanted to do was stretch it out. At that point we'd still had no idea whether we'd even make it back to The Woodlands safely. Not to mention what was going to happen to us next. For all I knew, we could've been ripped apart again within a matter of hours.

They were being so quiet all of a sudden, I wondered whether they might even be thinking that marrying Bastien so soon was a mistake.

I wanted to stay longer to talk through everything with them, but Brock arrived too soon, carrying a huge bulging backpack over his shoulders. We had to leave.

Bastien and I rose, and so did my parents. But before we could leave, my mother moved over to Bastien and took one of his hands in hers, before she looked him deep in the eye.

Then she turned to me, and to my relief, she finally smiled.

"I think you made a good choice, Vicky," she said softly. "And when you get back, we will give you both a proper wedding. Shade-style."

Bastien

Going to see Victoria's parents was more nerve-racking than I'd thought it would be. I felt vulnerable all of a sudden as they eyed me. I was the man who was taking their daughter away from them, whom they were expected to trust to keep her happy and safe for the rest of her life. Victoria's father especially had been sizing me up. And I would've done the same if I'd had a daughter as precious as Victoria.

But they seemed to approve of me in the end—or at least, Victoria's mother did. And for that I could only be grateful. Victoria and I had enough trouble from my side of the family to start receiving more from hers.

As we traveled back to the supernatural dimension from Earth, and then back to where we had left Mona outside Blackhall Mountain, my chest felt lighter than it had for a long, long time. In spite of the loss of Blackhall lives, and the fact that we still had my family to deal with, I couldn't shake the feeling that we might finally be nearing the end of the tunnel.

After all, Victoria and I were bonded already, and no matter what physical distance might be put between us, our hearts would remain as one.

Mona was waiting exactly where we had left her, a few feet in front of the line of frozen Mortclaws. She looked relieved to see us. I imagined it must be quite intimidating to be standing here alone guarding these beasts, even if she was a powerful witch.

Brock offloaded the backpack, which looked like it weighed a ton, and placed it gently on the floor in front of his mother.

"Thanks, Brock," she said, "and I'm glad you didn't take too long." She bent over the bag, unzipped it, and began rummaging through it. She murmured inaudibly as she dove deeper.

"Where do you plan to begin your experimentation?" I asked her. "I could take you to a room in the mountain."

"Yes," she said, "Good idea. Let's do that."

And so I led them into the mountain, to an empty chamber on the ground level which held a table and a few chairs. Mourning was underway now among the wolves, and most of them would be locked away.

Mona placed the bag on the floor, leaning it against one of the table legs before she began to offload its contents. I assumed that if she needed fire, she could manifest that on her own.

She retrieved the vial and placed it in front of her before lining up an array of glass bottles filled with multicolored and multi-textured ingredients, along with a mixing bowl.

"I'd like Brock to stay with me, but you two don't have to hang around here while I figure this out," she said. "I've no idea how long it will take."

I exchanged glances with Victoria. She shrugged.

"All right," I said.

"We will check in on you in a short while," Victoria added.

I looped her arm through mine and we headed out of the chamber and up through the mountain. I wanted to visit my quarters. We didn't pass a single wolf on the way as we climbed to the top floor. We moved through the apartment until we reached my bedroom, where we gazed out of the window at the rolling meadow below. She slipped her arms around me and leaned her head against my chest. I wondered what was going through her mind as she heaved a soft sigh.

I was contemplating my parents, naturally. Assuming that Mona managed to find a way to remove their brutality and unfair advantage over other werewolves, I wondered what would happen next. I was still officially the leader of the Blackhall tribe. They were still relying on me and yet, after everything, I didn't think that I could bring myself to uphold those duties here anymore. The Woodlands had brought only bad luck for Victoria and me so far, and now that we were married, I couldn't subject my wife to a long-distance relationship. If we survived this, I wanted to return to The Shade with her. Which meant that somebody among the Blackhalls was going to have to take up my post…

"Oh, what about Rona?" Victoria asked suddenly.

I felt a slight panic. Rona! I'd almost forgotten about her. She was still waiting for me in that old boat by the shore. I needed to go and retrieve her. Though she had been waiting so long already, I figured it was best to just wait a while longer to see what ended up happening with the Mortclaws. Then Victoria and I could go together to let her know the situation.

If Victoria hadn't mentioned her name exactly when she had, while I'd been in the middle of contemplating the future of the Blackhall tribe, it might never have even occurred to me that, of all the wolves who could possibly take up position as leader among the Blackhalls, Rona might just be the perfect candidate.

The Northstones were extinct now; she had nobody, and once she finally got out of that boat and returned to live on land, she would find herself all alone, with very few allies.

Yet she was the daughter of the two Northstone leaders. Leadership must run in her blood. Although I, too, was the son of leaders, it didn't come as naturally to me to command and lead. I suspected that Rona would do a good job in my place, and most importantly, I trusted that she would be a better woman than Brucella ever was. It seemed that she had taken after her father, Sergius, more than her mother and he had always been a decent man.

Victoria was probably also wondering what was going to happen to the Blackhall pack—whether I would still insist on staying to uphold my duties—but I held back on mentioning my idea about Rona just yet. I wanted to talk to Rona about it first, to see what her response would be, before raising Victoria's hopes for a solution.

"We'll go and find Rona soon—let's just wait a little longer and see how things play out with Mona," I replied, a little belatedly.

Then I'd have to hope that the Blackhalls would accept her as their leader...

Victoria and I waited together in my apartment for the next hour. We moved to the windows in my sitting room (whose windows had been fixed since Sendira smashed through them), which afforded us a view of the Mortclaws. I thought it might be interesting to watch them for a while, while Mona was working on her spell; perhaps we'd even start noticing some visible changes in them if she was on the right track. After a while, Victoria pulled me back to a wide, comfortable chair. She sat beside me and, her arms draping round my neck, kissed me tenderly.

"Whether or not Mona succeeds," she said softly as our lips parted, "we're going to find a way." She pressed her palm against my chest. "Nothing can keep us apart now."

I smiled at Victoria's serious gaze, still not quite believing that she was mine.

Her brows rose in question at my smile. "What?" she asked.

"Nothing, beautiful," I whispered, drawing her closer to me, "just keep kissing me."

We ended up spending some time lying in my bed together. We had too much on our minds to be in the mood for anything more than kissing, but there was something endlessly satisfying about simply lying with my mate, relishing the feel of her body close to mine, the way our forms melded. I could be in the middle of a storm, but Victoria made me feel at peace with the world.

Finally we made our way downstairs. Mona and Brock were still standing by the table, both of them gazing down into the mixing bowl which now held a brownish liquid, filled almost to the brim.

"How are things coming?" Victoria asked tentatively as we stood on one side of them.

Mona and Brock appeared to have been so absorbed in what they were doing they didn't even detect our entry until she had spoken.

"Oh," Mona murmured, pulling her eyes away from the mixture for but a moment. She inhaled. "Well, I can tell you that I've had no luck yet."

"You don't know that for sure," Brock told her. "We haven't even opened up the vial yet. We need to take a drop and test it to see how it reacts with what we're brewing up," he added on noticing our confused faces.

"We should be ready to test the first drop very soon though," Mona said, her eyes narrowing in concentration as she dipped down to sniff the concoction she was brewing.

I had no idea what all—or any—of the ingredients were

that Brock had brought back to her. And in all honesty, I didn't care. I wasn't interested in distracting the witches by asking them to explain their process; I just wanted to see the result.

We needed to solve this Mortclaw problem, once and for all.

DEREK

It was a shock for all of us to discover Field's true identity. I never could have imagined it in my wildest dreams. Yes, we'd suspected that the hunters had extracted some of River's eggs, but this… What chance was there of this? It had to be one in a million.

All I could think was that fate was on our side. If it weren't for Lawrence discovering Field and his four siblings, Grace would still be thrashing around on the hospital floor as a bloodsucking monster.

Sofia and I found out about Field after we had woken up and made our way to the hospital to check in on Grace. We found her and Lawrence, and she told us everything.

Now, I was hardly one to talk, given my history as a fire-spurting human… But, with the addition of Field, I couldn't help but think that our family was only getting stranger and stranger.

I could only imagine what a shock this must be for River to go through. And for my son. He suddenly found himself a surrogate father to a young man he hadn't even known existed a day ago. But I didn't have any doubt that he would adjust to support River. Their relationship was as solid as Sofia's and mine. They'd figure it out.

We stayed a while together in the hospital room before it was finally time to get down to business. Serious business. We had a mountain of work ahead of us, and we needed to start discussing order and strategy.

I called a meeting in the Great Dome. I made sure that Dr. Finnegan and the Hawks—or at least some of them—were invited to come, in addition to our regular council members. Everybody by now had already had ample opportunity to rest, so nobody should have an excuse not to attend.

Though, as the last of us piled into the building and took seats around the table, my brother was still noticeably absent.

But if there was anybody who had an excuse for not attending, it was him. He deserved to miss out on whatever our next mission was after the trauma he had been through in The Dewglades.

Thus, I found myself sitting at the head of the table with Sofia at my side. We had many deep issues to discuss now, but there was one smaller nagging issue that I wanted to get out of the way first before we sank ourselves deeper.

"The babies," I said, my eyes sweeping around my council. "We still haven't figured out what we are going to do with them. They can't live in the hospital forever. We have the ogres, the wolf cubs and then… those other things." My eyes fell on Safi. "Do you have any idea what those gray babies are?"

The jinni shrugged. "None of us do," she replied. "They are strange. Very strange. While the other babies cry and fuss, they hardly make a sound. Heck, they hardly even blink."

Creepy things…

"We haven't figured out what food they will eat yet either," she went on. "They've rejected everything we've tried to feed them so far—food that the ogres and the cubs have happily lapped up."

I inhaled through my nose. "All right," I said. "Well, let us first turn our attention to the three cubs and the two ogres. I am hoping that Bella and Brett will agree to adopt the latter..." At this point, I couldn't help but smirk internally. I was rather tempted to tie a ribbon around the more troublesome ogre baby, place him in a blanket-lined basket and leave him outside Lucas's door. "One of us should go and ask the ogres. And as for the wolf cubs—what are your thoughts?"

There was a pause before Micah, who sat next to his wife Kira, spoke up. "We will adopt one of them."

"Oh, good," I said, pleasantly surprised.

The next one came even more quickly. From Saira. "I'll take in one of the little snowflakes," she said.

Saira loved children, so that wasn't really a surprise.

I gazed around the room expectantly, waiting for the third taker. White, fluffy wolf cubs were hardly a tough sell... But I really was not expecting Aiden to suddenly call out, "Can you... give Kailyn and me a minute?"

"O-Of course," I said. I stared at them as they rose and headed swiftly out of the Dome.

I exchanged a glance with Sofia. Her eyes were sparkling with excitement, and the same surprise that I felt.

The couple returned a couple of minutes later, hand in hand, both with huge grins on their faces. "Derek," my father-in-law said, "Kailyn and I will take the third cub."

"Sold," I said, bringing a hand down against the table. "Good. So if we assume for now that Bella and Brett will

take the two ogres, then that leaves us with the gray babies…
Until we figure out what they are, I suppose they should
probably stay in the hospital."

We had no idea what kind of species they belonged to.
For all we knew, they could be dangerous. We would have
to do some investigation at some point in the future. Since
not a single person on the island knew what they were, we
would need to make a trip with them to The Sanctuary to
ask if anybody there knew. But none of this would happen
for some time, as we had to move on to more urgent matters
first.

"All right," I said, rubbing my hands together. "Moving
on… Let us talk about the antidote first. We have managed
to discover it thanks to Lawrence and Dr. Finnegan."
Lawrence was not here at present; he was still in the hospital
with my granddaughter. "We have figured out the mixture
that is required to cure the Bloodless disease and have
recorded Grace's entire transformation on camera—courtesy
of Xavier…"

Xavier nodded my way.

"But the first problem we face," I went on, "if we want to
stand any chance of distributing this antidote en masse, is
how do we replicate it? There are a number of issues. First,
we have only five vamp-Hawk boys—against who knows
how many thousands of Bloodless roaming America." *And*

other parts of the world. We had to make America our starting place, since that was the most severely affected.

"We have enough trees, so that is one ingredient solved," I said, "but then there are three other suspected plant-based ingredients." I looked to the Hawks among us, then to Corrine. "Corrine, I believe that you kept a sample of each of those ingredients, correct?"

"Yes," she said.

"Could you please fetch them now?" I asked her.

She vanished, and less than a minute later, she reappeared holding three almost empty test tubes.

"We suspect that these are plants from Aviary," she told the Hawks. "See if you can identify them by their smell."

She handed them to one of the Hawks, who sniffed each of the tubes before passing them to the others who had attended the meeting. Their brows lowered in thought.

"Well?" I asked. "Any idea?"

Killian, who'd been seated at the end of the line of Hawks and was still holding the tubes, said, "Definitely familiar."

"I have some ideas," Tidor added. "But we need to return to Aviary and do some investigation before getting your hopes up."

I feared that along with the trees, the hunters might have destroyed the rest of the ingredients, too. Though I found it hard to believe all of these other plants would also be isolated to that same area. It seemed too far-fetched. But there was no point in speculating.

"Will you return there now?"

The Hawks nodded, and rose. "Yes," Tidor said. "We will return and let you know our findings."

"Ibrahim." I addressed the warlock, sitting a few seats away from me. "Would you mind going with them? It will make transport much faster."

Ibrahim agreed.

"I suggest you take every single Hawk here on this island with you, in case you find the ingredients. If you do, you should bring as much back as possible."

The Hawks gathered round Ibrahim and a few moments later, all of them had vanished from the room.

Now, while we waited for their answer, we had other matters to discuss.

"How are we ever going to generate enough of this antidote?" I asked, directing my question at Dr. Finnegan, who sat with her young son at the other end of the table.

"Good question," Dr. Finnegan said. "One thing we do have on our side is that only a very small amount of each ingredient is required. You've seen the liquids up close, haven't you? They are all but transparent. Even the vial containing the blood—it wasn't even tinged red... now, I don't know how much blood those boys are able or willing to give up, and it's a stretch of the imagination to believe that we'll be able to cure every single Bloodless out there… all we can do is try to make the ingredients stretch as far as possible. It occurred to me that perhaps we could attempt to mix in some full Hawk blood, while still retaining the same effect. I don't know. I have to experiment. Full Hawk blood on its *own* doesn't work—that much we know."

"Okay," I said.

"So assuming that we manage to create a mass amount of antidote," Ben said, carrying forward my train of thought, "then what?"

I glanced at my son. I was sure that he already knew what would follow.

"Then we need to expose the IBSI," I said.

There was a span of silence as we all glanced at each other. There were a number of ways that we could go about this, and I had many ideas buzzing around in my head, but everything had to line up right, with the right timing, or we could find our actions backfiring on ourselves.

We began to discuss our options and potential strategies, along with all the things that could go wrong with each. It could be hard to come to a conclusion about anything when surrounded by so many—oftentimes conflicting—opinions. But after five hours, we managed to arrive at a plan we all agreed on. There were still potential holes in it—a number of potential holes—but those would always be there, no matter which route we chose…

Because dealing with the IBSI was never easy. And to combat what we had planned, I feared that Atticus Conway was going to put up the fight of his life.

BEN

My father, Xavier and I headed to the port to clear our heads and wait for the Hawks to return. In the meantime, Dr. Finnegan took Field and his brothers to the lab to begin experimenting with how to make their blood stretch as far as possible.

We strolled to the edge of the jetty and gazed out at the horizon. I remembered how, for so many months, IBSI ships had loomed outside our borders, floating in our waters and watching us.

Hopefully, soon a new dawn would break... a dawn without the IBSI.

They had been in power for so long, it was hard to even remember what the world had been like without their presence. But I could imagine how it would be... if everything went according to plan.

The three of us were tense as we waited. We had so much to get started on, but we couldn't do anything until the Hawks had returned and confirmed that they were able to find the ingredients. If they couldn't find them, all those hours of discussing and planning we had just been through would be for naught. Everything rested on us being able to manufacture the antidote on a meaningful scale.

When we caught sight of Ibrahim and a group of at least a hundred Hawks arriving further down the beach, I dared to get my hopes up. Especially as each of them was carrying large, bulging sacks. *Yes. Yes!* My father, Xavier and I raced toward them, hardly able to contain our relief.

"Did you discover all of them?" my father was the first to blurt out.

"We believe so," Ibrahim said, raising his own sack. "The Hawks located the three plants in a completely different part of Aviary—closer to where they had set up their residences."

Perfect.

We hurried to the Sanctuary and dumped the sacks in the courtyard. Ibrahim hurried to fetch Corrine and Dr. Finnegan and brought them outside. The two women began opening up the sacks, examining their contents. One of the plants was a kind of dark green weed, another a pale blue star-shaped flower, and the third a thorny deep-purple vine.

Corrine's eyes widened as she took in the mass of ingredients now piled up outside her front door. She blew out. "Okay... We're going to need containers. Very big containers."

* * *

Corrine and Dr. Finnegan quickly mixed up a potion using the new ingredients, along with an extract from the trees and the boys' blood, and tested it on one of the Bloodless Ibrahim still had locked up in their food cellar. As soon as the creature showed signs of turning—similar positive signs that Grace had shown—we could safely conclude that the plants worked.

Xavier, my father, Ibrahim and I exited the Sanctuary and returned to the sack-strewn courtyard. As we stood together, my father gripped my shoulder as well as Xavier's, looking us sternly in the eye.

"So you know what to do," he said.

Xavier and I glanced at each other, then nodded.

"And you, Ibrahim and Horatio," I said, "had better be punctual."

"I know," my father muttered. "I know."

As Ibrahim vanished with my father, they were supposed to stop at the Black Heights to pick up Horatio, and then the three of them were to depart from The Shade... Leaving the rest of us to pull together the rest of the puzzle.

First, Xavier and I headed to Eli and Shayla's apartment. We found Eli alone in his messy office. His hair was rumpled, glasses slightly askew as he slouched over his computer. He was editing footage—the footage of Grace turning into a human.

Xavier and I pulled up chairs and seated ourselves next to him, every harrowing detail playing before our eyes. This was not something that I wished to watch, but it was necessary.

"We have to trim it down so that it's not too long, but it must be enough to prove our point," Eli said, rubbing his forehead.

"I still worry that the broadcast station will say it's a fake," Xavier said, leaning forward tensely in his seat.

"Well," Eli said, turning to us with a dark expression in his eyes, "if all goes to plan, it won't matter."

Bastien

Victoria and I ended up wandering around for another hour, consistently checking in on the witches to keep up with their progress, until Mona and Brock announced— albeit with uncertain faces—that they had arrived at a solution they believed they were now ready to experiment with. Mona said that, assuming it worked as they intended, the new potion would interfere with the active nature of the elixir in a way that would smother it, rather than break it down… whatever that even meant.

Whatever the case, the idea was to dull the apparent life

of the elixir—which even now seemed to have something of a life of its own, even when it sat untouched on the table top. I noticed, for instance, on approaching it, it would start to swirl a little of its own accord. Victoria confirmed her own experience with the liquid when she'd tried to ingest only a tiny drop—but found much more leaping out onto her tongue.

This apparent liveliness of the liquid was what Mona believed she needed to still.

As she finished mixing up the brown liquid in her bowl, she eyed Victoria and me nervously.

"We've really got to hope this doesn't do any major damage," she muttered as she reached for the vial.

Opening its cap, she produced a spoon before tilting it ever so gently, pouring out a small amount of elixir. Then she produced a small clean glass bowl and tipped the elixir into it.

"Everyone watch it carefully," she said, as she set the bowl in the center of the table.

After about a minute, the small amount of elixir began to swirl in the depths of the bowl.

"So you see it moving now," Mona said. She dipped the spoon into her brown concoction and filled it in equal measure. She tipped it into the small glass bowl along with the elixir.

We watched with bated breath as a small hiss emanated from the bowl, followed by a small stream of smoke.

Mona kept it completely still for the next three minutes before she dipped the spoon in and mixed it more thoroughly together.

She removed the spoon, and we continued to stare at it.

Slowly, the mixture became still—recovering from Mona's stirring—but it did not begin to move again afterward, as the elixir on its own would have done. Not even the slightest bit of movement.

She picked up the bowl again and sniffed it, her nose curling. Brock sniffed it too.

"What are you thinking?" he asked his mother.

"I… I'm not sure," she replied, setting it still again on the table. "But it does seem like we've arrived at something. The only way to really know, of course, is to mix up the whole lot. I've only taken a tiny fraction of the vial's liquid so far. We now need to combine everything in the vial with our own liquid in equal measure."

She hesitated.

"What?" Victoria asked.

Mona shook her head. "I'm nervous about this."

If she was nervous, then Victoria and I definitely should be, given that we were directly in line to be affected if something went wrong. But I could hardly bring myself to feel afraid or nervous in the slightest. If anything, I just felt impatient now. I wanted Mona to mix it all together so we could see what happened. I hated all this suspense.

"I suggest we go outside for this," Mona said. "Then we can witness what's going on as it's happening."

"It'll be instant?" Victoria asked.

Mona clenched her jaw. "We'll see."

Brock carried the elixir, while Mona carried the brown substance. We headed by foot out of the mountain and approached the clearing, our eyes settling on the frustrated line of Mortclaws. The sun had reached them by now in their corner, and I imagined they were feeling incredibly hot and bothered. But this was a small punishment for all the lives and families they'd torn apart.

As they noticed us approach, they began to cause a ruckus again—most audibly, my mother. Demanding that they be freed, some even had the gall to threaten us. Not exactly the best strategy, given that Mona had the ability to keep them frozen as statues for as long as she felt like it.

We approached within six feet of them, where Mona and Brock paused. They set the two containers of liquid on the ground and knelt on the grass before them. I didn't miss the slight unsteadiness to Mona's hand as she unscrewed the vial. Given that the brown mixture's container was much larger, it seemed that she was going to tip all the elixir into it.

"You guys ready?" she muttered.

Ready for what? We had no idea. Victoria clutched my hand, even as we both said, "Yes."

"Just do it," I encouraged her.

"What are you doing?" Sendira shrilled.

What should have been done a long time ago, I felt like replying, but I bit my tongue. Mona needed to concentrate.

In one swift motion, she tipped the entirety of the vial into the brown substance and began to mix it rapidly. My hand around Victoria's tightened as a thin veil of smoke began to emanate from it, which soon became thick.

As five minutes passed, the Mortclaws grew more and more agitated to know what we were doing. Then, after ten minutes, they began to let out piercing howls. Their eyeballs bulged and if they had been able to move their bodies, I was sure that they would be thrashing about on the ground.

"Stop! Stop!" came the growls.

Then I felt a wave of nausea wash over me. Gripping Victoria's hand hard, I looked nervously at her.

"You feel anything?" I asked.

She clutched her forehead with her other hand. "Kind of dizzy," she murmured. Her forehead was breaking out in a sweat. My head felt hot, too.

I hoped the nausea would subside, and we wouldn't develop any worse symptoms.

The witches had risen to their feet by now, leaving the concoction on the ground, still billowing with smoke.

"You think it's working?" Victoria asked.

Mona gulped. "*Something's* working."

We dared to move closer. I hovered near my mother and father, watching as they experienced apparent agony. *Could this procedure kill them?* They looked to be in enough pain to be dying. I wasn't sure how that made me feel. As much as I wanted them out of my life, I couldn't say that I wanted them dead. They were still my parents, parents who had treated me the only way they knew how. My mother thought that she loved me. She thought that she was doing what was best for me and her family by arranging my marriage to Yuraya and keeping me away from Victoria. I couldn't bring myself to be so callous as to wish for their demise.

Finally, something more hopeful started to happen. My nausea began to subside, and Victoria confirmed the same for her. But more importantly, each of the Mortclaws—who had been in their giant wolf forms, Mona having caught them in the midst of an attack—before our very eyes, were starting to shrink. Slowly but surely, their oversized limbs began to retract on themselves, grow slimmer, shorter. After half an hour, every one of them was down to a normal size— or a relatively normal size for a werewolf. They were still large, but the Mortclaws were a naturally large breed; they had been large even before the black witches had gotten hold of them. This new size they were adopting was certainly explainable.

I once again looked at Victoria, and I caught her looking at me too. We were searching each other for external changes. Neither of us saw anything different.

As we resumed our attention on the Mortclaws, I realized that something else was starting to happen now. Their limbs were mutating. Tails shrinking. Paws thinning. They were assuming their humanoid forms.

Of course. It's daytime. That meant that they were losing their ability to shift at will. They must be humanoid during the daytime, wolf at night, just like the rest of the werewolves in The Woodlands.

Mona, her son and Victoria all looked to me at once. I knew what they were thinking, because I was thinking exactly the same thing. *Does this mean that I have lost my ability to switch at will, too?*

I must have.

I tried to assume my wolf form now, and what had previously been as effortless as blinking, I found I was unable to do, no matter how much I willed the transformation. I was stuck as a humanoid and I would be until tonight. This revelation brought about an unexpected twinge in my chest. I felt disappointed, saddened to have lost this ability. I'd taken it for granted for most of my life and indeed, it had been useful on more occasions than I could count. It had given me a freedom that other wolves couldn't enjoy. Still, I could hardly feel too upset about it, given the miracle that was happening to my family before my very eyes.

It was hard to really tell when a wolf was disheveled, given that they looked like wild beasts anyway. But as all of the Mortclaws were forced back into the humanoid forms, each of them looked like they had been dragged backward through the woods—their hair sticking out at odd places, their breathing unregulated, and each of them... naked.

The four of us quickly looked away, facing Blackhall Mountain.

I guessed that this marked the completion of their transformation, or rather, de-transformation. No longer the extraordinary beasts who used their powers for evil, I imagined it would take a long time for them to get used to being fallible again. And they had made enemies out of every single werewolf who roamed The Woodlands. They would have to watch out; it wouldn't surprise me if, once others found out, they'd band together to attack the Mortclaws out of revenge.

But these were the seeds the Mortclaws had sown. Be it their fault or not that they craved werewolf flesh, it didn't vanish the fact that they were going to have to face the consequences of their actions. They had better watch their backs.

Time to finally wake up to reality.

Victoria

As I accompanied Bastien to Blackhall Mountain to fetch some clothes for his family (this was Bastien's wish—in spite of all they'd done, he wished to treat them with at least this basic civility), I couldn't find words to express my relief. Assuming that Mona's procedure had done its work already, Bastien and I were okay. We had survived it. And the Mortclaws were back to their original state.

As for the diluted elixir, Mona said that she would carry it back to The Shade with us and keep it somewhere safely in her spell room.

"See if you can still fly," Bastien told me, as we neared the mountain entrance.

I found myself filled with trepidation as I attempted to rise.

I couldn't.

Disappointment gripped me. I had been hoping that I might be able to keep that power. I had become a kind of Superwoman. I supposed that my increased strength would've gone now too… and my speed. *Bummer.* It was a shame I'd never gotten the chance to explore the full extent of the powers I had adopted—it really would have been cool if I had the ability to shoot lasers from my eyes. *Oh, well.* That ship had sailed.

I couldn't feel too sore, just as I doubted Bastien felt too sore about losing his own exceptional abilities.

As far as I understood Mona's procedure, the elixir was still active but in some kind of neutralized state—diluted by whatever that other brownish substance that she had mixed it with was. I doubted that there would be any way to restore the elixir to its former state, even if it did somehow get into the wrong hands. Mona had mixed the bowl thoroughly.

Although everyone in the mountain was mourning—and this was something that werewolves needed to be left alone for—Bastien couldn't help but yell out, "The Mortclaws are no longer the monsters they were! The spell has been broken.

They are outside now, you can see for yourselves!"

This captured the attention of dozens of werewolves. They poked their heads out of their doors as we passed, many of them even leaving the corridors and making their way to the exit.

Once we had gathered enough clothing, we hurried back out and laid a set of clothes in front of each of the Mortclaws, whom Mona still had frozen and immobile. I didn't pay much attention to male and female clothing, though I tried not to give any men a dress.

As I glanced back at the entrance, it looked like the news had quickly spread throughout the entire mountain and everybody was crowding out to witness the scene.

Bastien looked at Mona. "Do you think it's safe to release the spell now?" he asked.

Mona shrugged. "I'm pretty sure that it's as safe as it will ever be. I wanted to wait for you to see if you are ready."

Bastien nodded. "Yes, I think I'm ready."

As Mona lifted her spell, there was a scurry among each of the Mortclaws, snatching up clothes angrily and dressing themselves before they all stood to their full height.

They looked like they wanted to run at Mona and attack, but after being frozen and unable to move a single limb for gods knew how many hours, they were hardly about to charge at her.

Instead, they snarled and hissed curses. Then Bastien's mother stepped forward and approached him, Bastien's father behind her.

Bastien's arm immediately shot to me and shoved me behind him. I had to remind myself that I could no longer fly away, as I had been able to do when escaping Yuraya. I had to scrub that boldness from my system from now on, or I could find myself getting into big trouble.

I was the human girl again... at least until, maybe, I decided to turn into a vampire like my parents.

Sendira and her husband stopped two feet away from us. She stared into the eyes of her son, searching, as though a part of her still disbelieved that Bastien had allowed this to happen to them.

"And where do we stand now, Bastien?" she asked, her voice deep and scratchy.

Bastien's brows lowered in a deep frown. "Where do you think we stand? I can give you one hint: it's not on the same side."

She pursed her lips, swallowing hard. Bastien's words had hurt her.

"You, Father, and the rest of your pack can do whatever you want now," Bastien went on, "Though I suggest that you be careful and tread lightly," he added in a lower tone. "You haven't exactly gone out of your way to make friends in this land."

I wouldn't have been surprised if the Mortclaws were forced to leave The Woodlands now. I would've thought that it would be incredibly dangerous for them to stay here. I could imagine a huge army of wolves banding together and attacking them at night while they slept, finishing them off for all the lives that they had claimed. But that wasn't Bastien's or my concern anymore.

Bastien's arm wrapped around my waist and he pulled me closer to him. "As for my mate and I," he went on, "I don't think you deserve to know our plans for the future, considering all you've done to try to tear us apart."

Sendira's eyes moistened. I couldn't help but feel a slight twinge in my chest as she choked, "Don't discard me, Bastien. Please."

Bastien's jaw tensed, but he remained unswayed. He stepped backward even as his mother moved forward, attempting to hold his hand.

He cleared his throat. "Maybe, at some point in the future, we will meet again. Maybe, I will allow you to meet our children. But these are all maybes. If you want to have anything to do with me again, you will need to prove that you have changed—every single one of you—and given up the ways and attitude of the black witches."

With that, Bastien drew further away from his parents.

Taking me with him, we returned to Mona and Brock's side.

"Goodbye," he told them.

It seemed that Sendira had finally gotten the message that she had been cut out of the picture—there was no use in her still trying to cling on to her son. Bastien had forsaken her, his father, and the rest of the clan. Now, they had to turn their thoughts to survival in this suddenly hostile world.

After one last longing glance at their son, Sendira and her husband turned slowly, before they and the rest of the Mortclaws in mismatched clothing hurried into the woods. Sendira hadn't even bothered to cast me a final look.

I searched Bastien's face as they disappeared through the trees. It was stoic, though behind his eyes were many emotions. I was sure that he felt guilt, but his behavior was actually for their benefit in the long term. Sendira couldn't just think that she could act however she wanted and there would be no consequences in regards to her and her son's relationship. She had to think long and hard, and redeem herself—*stop being another Brucella*—if she ever wanted to have a relationship with him again.

After being at the mercy of that woman's temperament, I could see how empowering it was for Bastien to put her in her place. My heart soared for him as I gave his hand a reassuring squeeze.

He glanced down at me, his expression warming. He

scooped me up in his arms, lifting my feet from the ground and kissing me deeply.

We both knew what the Mortclaws' retreat meant for us now.

Finally, we were free.

Bastien

Although we were now free from the Mortclaws, I was not yet free of my responsibilities in The Woodlands. First, I had to finally go and fetch Rona. Poor girl, she had been hiding for days.

"So what's happening now?" Mona asked, her voice audibly tired. She couldn't know how much I appreciated all that she had done for Victoria and me. There was no way that either of us could repay her. But I needed to request her kindness and patience for just a little longer.

"I need to go and retrieve Rona Northstone. She is waiting in a boat by the shore for me. Then I need to have a meeting with my people. If you would be so kind as to hold on…"

Mona and Brock agreed, and I was just about to transform into my wolf form when I remembered that I could no longer do that.

Mona offered to transport us to the shore to make things faster and I eagerly accepted. Thus the four of us, Victoria, Brock, Mona and I, headed to the shoreline where I had stashed Rona.

I raced along the dock looking for the boat, when I reminded myself that I could shout out for her now. There was no need to hide any longer. "Rona! Rona!" I called, even as I found and leapt onto her boat.

"Bastien?" her timid voice called up from the lower deck.

We met halfway on the staircase. She was looking bedraggled, to say the least. And she was probably hungry. I doubted she would have had much opportunity to look for food, given my instruction to stay in the boat at all possible times.

Her face lit up as I said, "Everything is solved. You can come out now."

I couldn't bring her family back to life—nor would I, in all honesty, wish to bring Brucella back to life even if I could—but I could try to introduce her to a new life, one that would hopefully be satisfying for her.

"Come with me to Blackhall Mountain," I said, leading

her away from the boat and onto the dock where the others were waiting for me.

The witches magicked us back to the mountain, where I immediately led everyone inside.

"What's going on?" Rona asked, looking utterly bewildered.

Before answering any questions, I took her first to the kitchens. I told her to help herself to food. Once she had gathered what she wanted—there was still fresh food from earlier in the day—I sat her down at a table, watching as she began to hungrily eat.

"I want to offer you a place here in Blackhall Mountain," I told her, seeing no reason to beat around the bush. "as the Alpha of the Blackhall pack. Assuming that my pack agrees, you could make this your home, your new family. For as long as you wanted."

I paused, gauging her action. She had stopped eating and was now staring at me, jaw slackened.

"I think that you would be a better leader than me," I went on, "and I'm sure that you'll find the accommodations comfortable, and my people welcoming, once you got to know them... What do you say?"

She set down her fork, still gaping. "Bastien," she murmured, eyeing him uncertainly. "This is... a huge responsibility. I am not even a Blackhall. I am a Northstone.

Even if I were to accept, what makes you think anybody would wish for me to rule?"

"Because it will be on my recommendation. My people trust me, just as they trusted my parents... and I trust you. Leadership is in your blood. There is no other werewolf in my tribe who wishes to rule."

"I don't understand why you don't want this position," Rona said. "It's what your parents would have wanted, isn't it? I mean, your foster parents."

I smiled, melancholy filling me as I thought of my Blackhall parents. "I think that they would have wanted me to be happy," I replied. I reached out for Victoria's hand and clasped it in mine.

Rona raised a brow. "You... You and—"

I finished her sentence. "Yes, Victoria and I are mated now. And I wish to spend some uninterrupted time in her world... Hence, I am asking this favor of you."

Rona exhaled slowly, her eyes lowering to her plate in thought. Then, to my surprise, she asked, "Is Jax still here... unmated?"

"Jax? Yes... unmated."

A blush rose to her cheeks. *Oh, my... All this time, Rona's had an eye for Jax.* He was Cecil's grandson, an amiable blond-haired man a little older than me. I could understand why any girl would take a liking to him, but... Rona? I'd never known. And something told me that if Brucella wasn't dead, I would never have known. Rona had been told all her life by her mother that her betrothed was already chosen for her, and he—I—would make himself known to her when he was ready to commit to marriage. Rona's eyes weren't supposed to have strayed to any man during that time; she was supposed to have remained chaste… but apparently, Jax had caught Rona's eye on her visits here over the years.

My confirmation that Jax was still available evidently made my proposal a whole lot more compelling to her. In fact, it seemed to seal the deal.

She sighed. "All right… If your people will have me here, then I'll try it."

"Good," I said, rising to my feet. "I don't think you'll regret this decision."

I decided to leave Rona to finish her meal while I went to talk to the rest of the wolves about my plans. I left Victoria, Mona and Brock with her and began running about the mountain, calling a meeting. Soon enough, everybody was gathered in the court. I took a seat on my—or rather, my Blackhall father's—throne for what I believed might be the last time.

"Since not one of you wishes to lead or feels capable of leading our tribe forward into the future, and since I am now married"—I paused as murmurings of surprise swept around the room—"to Victoria," I added—"I have come up with a solution. Every one of you should be familiar with Rona Northstone." *Or at least have heard of her.*

I gazed around at the sea of nodding heads.

"Well, she is the only surviving member of the Northstone clan since the Mortclaws attacked them, much like they attacked us. Unless and until one of you decides to step forward and take on the responsibility, I propose that Rona lead you forward henceforth, while I am gone in The Shade. I have already spoken to her and she is willing. Now all that remains is for you to accept."

Rona had always been the quiet sort—she had never really done or said anything that could attract hate or dislike from the Blackhalls. There were no real objections raised. Everybody seemed quite neutral—not exactly excited, but neutral. Then, one by one, they agreed.

They trusted my gut instinct about Rona. And I figured that they were right to do so because it was rarely wrong. It was difficult to hoodwink me into trusting somebody; I sensed insincerity from miles away.

There were accompanying questions, of course, like when she would arrive and take on her duties, and would I ever return? I explained to them that Rona had arrived already and was just having a meal but I would introduce her shortly. As for would I ever return, of course I would. The

Woodlands was my home… just not for a while.

I hurried down to fetch Rona from the kitchens to find that she had finished her meal by now and was in conversation with Brock, Mona and Victoria.

"I've spoken to my people," I told her. "They are willing to accept you into our midst, at least, on a trial basis at first."

I took her along with the others into the court where the wolves were waiting, and introduced her as the new chieftain.

Rona's eyes wandered the crowd, and I knew who she was searching for. She soon found Jax, standing tall at the back of the crowd. I looked at Cecil, who was clapping. I was glad that he seemed to be approving of my nomination.

Thus, after officially placing the crown upon Rona's head and telling Cecil that he would be her advisor from now on, I stayed for a little longer to watch the interaction between Rona and her new people as they mingled and introduced themselves. And then I felt that my job here was done.

We could finally return to The Shade.

Ben

We waited with Eli for the next half hour, and once he'd finished editing the footage, he transferred it to a thumb drive along with the unedited reel and placed it in a backpack. Then we returned to the Sanctuary to see how much progress Corrine and Dr. Finnegan—and Shayla, who had joined them—had made in creating more of the antidote. We didn't need a lot initially, just one backpack's worth of tubes.

The witches and the scientist had it already prepared and distributed into tubes when we showed up. Corrine placed them in Eli's backpack, along with syringes.

"Aisha is figuring out some storage solutions for the antidote," Corrine said, "while Dr. Finnegan works to create more with Safi. So if you're ready, let's fetch Lawrence."

We headed to my daughter's room in the hospital, where we found Lawrence sitting with her. Lawrence hadn't attended the meeting in the Dome, so I explained to him our plan now and asked if he would come with us. Given that he had such an intimate connection with the IBSI, his presence was important to our plan, so I was relieved when he agreed to come… Though I hadn't exactly expected him to refuse. He was doing this for his mother as much as for the rest of the world.

I kissed my daughter's cheeks and hugged her goodbye before we left her alone, taking Lawrence to the Port. Standing on the jetty, we went over what we had discussed in the Great Dome earlier to make sure we were all on the same page, and then we departed by magic.

Once our feet touched the ground again, we were standing on a long, broad street at the foot of a gray-tinted glass building that spanned thirteen floors. We were in a protected residential area of Chicago, the other side of the wall that marked the boundary of Bloodless territory.

This building was Chicago's primary broadcasting station—one of America's primary stations, too, and probably the most heavily influenced by the IBSI's agenda.

It was only a few miles away from the IBSI's headquarters itself. Lights glowed in the windows on most floors. Leaving the others, I thinned myself and entered the plush reception room in search of a map of the building. It wasn't difficult to find. I found one pinned up against the wall opposite the reception desk.

I soon verified that the tenth floor was where we needed to head. I returned to my companions and informed them, before the witches transported us up through the building.

We arrived outside of an elevator, which led us to the entrance of a glass-walled room that spanned the entire floor. It was filled with people milling about, scattered desks, phones and computers, and at the far end were cameras and other recording equipment, along with a studio setup.

Nobody had noticed us yet and nobody would… until it was too late.

I gripped the handle of the door and pushed it wide open for us to step inside.

The noise of the door drew eyes in our direction but before anyone could react, Shayla and Corrine sent paralyzing curses bounding about the room, until everyone had been frozen in their positions.

We moved deeper inside, gazing around at everybody's stunned faces—they were particularly shocked to see Lawrence.

"We mean you no harm," I spoke up, "but we have something to show you. Something that you all must watch."

Eli withdrew the thumb drive from his backpack while my eyes settled on a large screen that extended across an entire wall.

"Would somebody set up this screen for us?" I asked, lifting up the thumb drive.

Corrine lifted the spell from one of the men standing near us, and as he regained control over his limbs, he immediately darted for the door. I ran after him and grabbed him, holding him back.

"Please," I told him firmly.

Seeing that there was no way out of my grip, he gulped before scurrying over to one of the computers. I hovered over him with Eli and planted the thumb drive on the desk next to him. The man picked it up with shaking hands before plugging it in.

As the screen flickered on and the footage began to play, I looked to Corrine. "You need to give everyone control of their necks and faces," I told her. Not all of them were even looking directly at the screen but in the opposite direction.

"Certainly," Corrine said, before obliging.

The screen flickered and Eli's edited tape began to play. I kept my focus on everyone's reaction as they watched.

All of them looked more and more shocked as the tape

progressed, their jaws slackening. Nobody spoke a word until the reel came to an end.

"What you have just witnessed," I said, "is the Bloodless antidote in action. We have discovered a cure that the IBSI has fought to keep hidden for more than a decade."

"H-How do we know this tape is even real?" one of the men spluttered. "It looks like it could be a product of special effects."

I furrowed my brows at the bearded man, who, judging from the badge fixed to his shirt, was the department's manager.

"I'm sure you all recognize me," Lawrence said, stepping forward. "The man the IBSI proclaimed to be dead. That organization has spouted nothing but lies since the day it was founded… and you all have been nothing but their obedient pawns, broadcasting their lies to the world. If anything is fake, it's every single news story you've run on behalf of the IBSI for the past few decades."

"But if you really think this could be a fake," I said, "then we can prove it to you. You can witness a transformation before your very eyes."

This man—and other doubtful faces in this room—would soon regret his skepticism.

"You and a cameraman are going to accompany us on a trip," I said, "whether you like it or not."

I looked to Corrine and nodded. We all knew what to do now. Shayla would stay behind to hold the fort with Eli, while the rest of us would travel to the shadows of Bloodless Chicago.

BEN

Corrine made us appear on the road outside the crematorium laboratory, which appeared to have been abandoned. There were no vehicles in the parking lot, no smoke emanating from the chimneys. We immediately set about the task of scouting Bloodless— we wanted three of them to prove beyond all doubt that the antidote was real. Corrine didn't have much trouble in gathering them. The first one, a short creature, was hanging out near the lab's gates. Corrine froze it and lowered it onto the ground in front of us. She found two more Bloodless in the street parallel to us, and positioned them next to the first—laying all of them on their backs.

Then Corrine rummaged in the backpack and drew out the antidote along with three syringes. According to Dr. Finnegan, the cure did not have to be swallowed, but could be injected, too. There would be less likelihood of waste by injection rather than pouring it into their mouths and hoping that they swallowed as easily as Grace had.

"Get your camera rolling," Lawrence demanded of the cameraman. Once the man had acquiesced, one by one, Corrine injected the Bloodless.

The cameraman's hands were shaking. Both he and the manager looked absolutely terrified to be here on this side of the wall. They were mere humans after all. As the turning process began, it wasn't long before a group of Bloodless came loping our way. Corrine put up a protective shield around us before they could get close, giving us peace of mind while we waited for the transformation to complete.

The two news station employees watched in awe as the Bloodless changed more and more, until finally they were recognizable as humans. Broken and battered, but humans nonetheless.

The first Bloodless we had found turned out to be a short young woman, while the other two were men, perhaps in their late twenties.

They all appeared to be in far worse shape than Grace had

been in. Their noses looked like they might never recover, and their skin was dry and peeling. I supposed this was because they had been Bloodless longer than my daughter had, and evidently, conditions here on this side of the wall were far worse than the sheltered conditions Grace had been kept in.

The turned humans were so weak they could hardly raise their heads, and they lay, panting on the ground, their eyes half closed in pain.

"So now you've seen it for yourself," Lawrence announced. "You have seen and recorded the cure in action."

The two employees were dumbstruck, even as the cameraman lowered his camera.

"And now you have no excuse not to cooperate with us in reporting this news," I told them sternly. Of course, we had them trapped in that room, and we could've forced them to make the broadcast. But I wanted them to see it for themselves, to no longer be hoodwinked by the IBSI.

The two men nodded, though they looked terrified. There was a different type of terror in their eyes now—more dread and fear. They feared the truth, and what broadcasting it would do to them. But as we would hopefully show them in the hours to come, no matter how tangled a web of lies was woven, truth always triumphed in the end.

BEN

We rushed back to the broadcasting station, bringing the three turned humans with us. We arrived to find Shayla still maintaining order—not that there was much order to maintain. Everybody in the room was still frozen.

We laid the three humans on the ground before Corrine suggested, "Shayla, now that I'm back to retake control, why don't you go and take these poor humans back to the hospital in The Shade? Find somebody to help them, leave them there and return."

"Good idea," Shayla murmured, even as she eyed the humans. Then she vanished with them, leaving us to our next task.

Recording that footage had taken guts on the part of the cameraman and the manager, but this next step would take a whole lot more.

Corrine glanced around the room at the frozen statues. "If I release the spell, can I trust you all to behave yourselves?" she asked.

They responded with murmurs of *yes*. I didn't trust any of them, however, so before Corrine removed the spell, Xavier and I stood at each of the exits—the main exit leading to the elevator, and another, on the other side of the floor, which was a fire exit.

Corrine relinquished her magic while Lawrence took center stage and began to command the employees.

They moved to the studio and began preparations for a broadcast. I caught many of them glancing wistfully at the exits—clearly none of them wanted to have anything to do with this. They feared the IBSI would make them regret it, but it was time that they all grew some balls.

Ten minutes later, they were ready to roll.

They projected the footage on a large screen as Lawrence took his place in front of the cameras. He began to introduce himself as the man who was proclaimed to be dead by the IBSI, and proceeded with the story of the IBSI's deceit. I couldn't help but feel a swell of pride for Lawrence—pride that I was sure his mother would have felt—as he looked determinedly, steely, into the camera.

But Lawrence barely got halfway through the broadcast before an explosion shook the building. Somewhere above us, a bomb had detonated, causing a resounding tremor that ran through the walls and floors. The lights buzzed and flickered out.

Being furthest away, I didn't have time to make it to the witch as she gathered everyone in the room together. I thinned myself and rose up through the crumbling levels, passing through smoke and then fire, until I broke out into the open night sky. I spotted the rest of our group as they landed a few miles off, on the roof of a different building. I touched down next to them and we all turned back and stared at the smoking skyscraper... and then at the black helicopter hurrying away above it.

I hadn't expected the IBSI to respond quite like that. I'd thought that perhaps the fact that we were on live television would cause them to handle the situation more delicately, if they could figure out how to handle it at all. But we were all stupid to think that they would've done anything but respond with violence.

At least we had all gotten out, and as shaken as we were, I couldn't help but experience satisfaction as the helicopter buzzed in the sky like an angry wasp. We had unsettled

Atticus.

But our work was not done yet. Not nearly done. We had not been able to complete the broadcast. We had not been able to show the entire transformation, and Lawrence was unable to finish all that he had to say.

Which meant that we needed to move to another station, far away from here to throw the IBSI off, and quickly.

We waited on the roof of the building for a few minutes for Shayla, not wanting to leave her abandoned. Corrine spotted her emerging in the sky near the damaged building—no doubt staring down in shock—as escapees piled out from the ground-floor exit. I wondered how many innocent lives the IBSI had just claimed from those who had been on the upper floors. This was no joke anymore. No joke indeed.

Once Corrine returned with Shayla, who heaved a huge sigh of relief to see us all safe—including her husband Eli—we needed to discuss our next destination.

"I would say New York," Lawrence said, looking to the manager for his opinion.

The manager looked too shellshocked for words, but he nodded weakly.

"All right," Corrine said, gathering us together. "New York it is."

It was déjà vu as we arrived outside another skyscraper. After figuring out the appropriate location in the building, we took over the room in much the same way as we had overtaken the Chicago station.

Eli had fortunately had the presence of mind to disconnect all the footage and grab it before we left Chicago so that we could continue.

But the IBSI had a base in New York, too. We could not be so careless in our approach this time. They might have thought that they'd destroyed Lawrence—perhaps they had not known that he had been accompanied by a witch—but the moment they picked up on us broadcasting the news via a different channel, they would target that too.

"We need to keep watch," Corrine said.

"More than just keep watch, we need protection," I added.

The dragons would have come in handy for this, but we didn't have the patience to wait for them to arrive right now. Thus, Shayla headed outside, promising to keep watch on the skies and use her magic to ward off any approaching helicopters.

Hopefully, there wouldn't be too many at once, and she could deal with them all without problems.

And so began our second broadcast. This time, as

A DAY OF GLORY

Lawrence began to address the camera with the Bloodless footage playing in the background, Eli filmed it with his phone—which was a good idea. I already had plans for what we would do with that footage once Eli had finished recording.

We got further into the broadcast this time, although I eventually heard the faint whirring of choppers. And then came another explosion, except this time, the building did not shake. The bomb had not reached the structure. Shayla had managed to somehow avert it and hopefully now she would ward the aircraft away.

We needed to be quick nonetheless. I guessed that they would send backups. There was only so far that Shayla's attention and strength could stretch.

I clenched my fists nervously as I watched Lawrence plough on unwavering with his story, until finally he had finished and they had displayed all the highlights from the footage marking the various stages of the Bloodless-to-human transformation.

Lawrence ended with a gleam of passionate triumph in his eyes. "Although the IBSI is clearly not qualified to be in the position of authority they currently assume, there are others who are. The Shadow League, a cooperation of supernaturals you might've heard mentioned, are in the process of bringing the IBSI down. We will establish a new order, based on

134

honesty and diligence. For years you have had the wool pulled over your eyes by the IBSI—but now it's time to take it off. Embrace the truth, and soon we will all be living it."

With that, the broadcast cut. I would've been extremely nervous if it had gone on any longer.

"Okay, guys, we should get out of here now," I said.

The humans among us—both the Chicago and New York employees—looked panicked as the explosions grew louder. Corrine gathered everyone together, before transporting them safely out of the building.

I preferred to make my own way out, as I had done last time. I rose up through the floors and spotted two black helicopters attempting to shatter the building. Shayla, breaking out in a sweat, was managing to keep them at bay with a giant protective shield around the building.

Anger rising in my veins, I soared upward until I was level with the choppers. I yelled at the men in the bellies of the aircrafts: "Stop bombing! Your targets are no longer in the building! We have finished the broadcast..." *And soon, we will finish you.*

Ben

We headed to a different side of New York City, where we allowed all the employees we had gathered to trickle away if they wanted to. But none of them felt safe without us now, so they opted to remain under our—or rather, our witches'—protection.

As we touched down in a quiet back street, Eli uploaded the footage he had taken on his phone to the most popular news sites on the internet. Word should spread quickly from here as the people took over propagating the message.

And in the meantime, there was more that we could do to send our message further. Broadcast it via more news stations. We already had over fifty employees with us. By the time we were done, we might have accumulated a whole army.

We asked the Chicago manager where he suggested we head next; he said Los Angeles would be a good port of call.

And so we followed his advice, pulling the same trick with Shayla watching the building on arrival. But we weren't so lucky here as we had been in New York. We only managed to get through half of the broadcast before the electricity abruptly went out.

We tried in two more cities, San Francisco and Houston—where we thankfully had more success. Perhaps the IBSI were less organized in these cities, but we managed to get through the full broadcast.

I was going to suggest that we travel to other parts of the country when Eli checked his phone and reported to us that the video had already gone viral.

The people were indeed hungry for the truth.

I gazed down triumphantly at the rapidly rising video views and articles popping up all over the web. Soon, we would be reaching people in the millions.

We landed in a quiet park and took a pause to recalibrate.

"I think we've done what we can," Eli murmured, still scrolling through his phone. "It's spreading like wildfire."

I agreed. We had completed the first step of our plan—

shake the IBSI's almost holy public perception and create widespread doubt in the organization... Now we had to discuss what was next.

Atticus

My drink slipped from my hand as I scrolled through the rapidly increasing number of blogs and news sites picking up Lawrence's story.

His broadcasting it via the television was bad enough. As soon as I'd gotten wind that my son had infiltrated a Chicago news station, I had feared that he would blast out his misguided message on the internet too, just as he had previously threatened me he would.

That boy has really crossed the line now. Really crossed it. There is no returning from this.

Any leniency I might have showed him while he had been with us in Canada had been a mistake. I should've treated him as the person he was, a traitor just like his mother.

My softness had been my mistake. *One would have thought I'd learned by now...*

I sank back in my chair in front of my desk, gripping my phone hard in my hands.

So the League really thinks they have what it takes to replace us. They really want our power? They really think they'd know how to use it...

After I mulled over the situation for the next five minutes, I decided that I would give it to them.

I would play them at their own game.

BEN

We had begun to discuss our next move when Eli, who had been keeping an eye on the constantly spreading news, interrupted us, panic shining in his eyes.

"Oh, no," he rasped.

"What?" I urged.

"The boundaries in Chicago separating the residences from the Bloodless... they have fallen. They have been *blown*."

I grabbed the phone from him and stared down at the report. Horror filled me as I realized what was happening. I looked to Lawrence, who appeared to be thinking the same thing.

"My father," he muttered. "I'm sure of it."

"*Why* is he doing this?" Xavier posed.

"I should've realized this was what my father would do," Lawrence said, cursing beneath his breath. "It's just so typical of him. He wants to make a public mockery of us, after I just declared that TSL's plan is to take over. They want to prove to the world how incompetent we are at the jobs they are carrying out—like keeping the divide between Bloodless and humans."

My throat constricted as I imagined hordes of Bloodless flooding into towns inhabited by families and children. We had our work cut out as it was, attempting to cure the existing Bloodless, let alone thousands more who were probably being created as we spoke.

Eli took the phone back from me and continued scrolling. "Oh, great," he said, "apparently IBSI Chicago has made a statement, confirming that they are withdrawing even the mutants. And they will do the same in New York, very soon."

"Scare tactics!" Xavier fumed.

And they were working. I could only imagine how terrified the humans who lived in the city must be. Or humans who lived anywhere that was dependent on the IBSI's protection.

It seemed that we had pushed the IBSI to the point of desperation, and they were no longer cautious enough to hide their ugly side publicly, for this was nothing but open blackmail. Continue on our path, and they were going to continue wreaking havoc on the cities and townships that they were supposed to be protecting. If anybody ever had any doubts about the IBSI's motives being tainted by power, they should be eradicated now. And yet it didn't matter. Because the irrefutable fact remained: the people still needed the IBSI to keep the Bloodless sectioned off.

We still needed them. We weren't prepared yet to take their place—and they knew it, which was why they had withdrawn just at the wrong time. I had honestly been hoping that they would remain clinging to power as long as possible, and if anything, increase their protection around the cities to prove themselves to be more competent than us. But apparently, I still had a lot to learn about Mr. Atticus Conway, and Lawrence knew a lot more about him than me.

We had little time left until the IBSI were going to do the same to New York... and then where next? When would they stop, or would they even stop?

We had done our job in unsettling Atticus, that much was clear. We had done that job too well.

BEN

First, we all traveled together to the borders of Chicago, and then the witches transported everyone to The Shade, while I remained behind.

In this state of emergency, any plans had to be scrapped. Our first priority had to be to gather as large an army as we could possibly muster from our island and for all of them to rush back to Chicago to try to remedy the situation—including the dragons. They also needed to bring as much antidote from the island as they could carry—I hoped that Dr. Finnegan and her helpers would be prepared for what we required.

In the meantime, Lawrence suggested that I go to search

for Atticus. If the order to blow the boundaries had come from Chicago HQ, Lawrence was sure that it would be his father directly behind it... which meant that Atticus was likely back in Chicago. I had to search for him and attempt to stop him from giving another order. He had seconds and thirds and fourths in command, who would not respond to Atticus's absence lightly—assuming I did get hold of him. If he'd already discussed his plans with them, likely my capturing Atticus would make no difference; they'd go through with them anyway. But hunting down that man was the most useful thing that I could think to do with my time right now, and so, after the others vanished, I dashed toward the looming silhouette of the IBSI's Chicago headquarters. The boundaries sectioning their compound off from the rest of the city remained intact, keeping the Bloodless out, not that this should come as a surprise.

As I passed through the main entrance building, I tried to block out images of the horrific situation going on around me in the city and focus on the man who had started it all.

Lawrence had better be right that he was here in Chicago.

I headed straight for Atticus' office, whose location I knew well enough by now. But it was empty. As was the rest of his apartment. I continued to search throughout the rest of the buildings, until I lost patience completely at one point and manifested myself before a hunter, pinning him against a wall and threatening him for an answer. But I made no progress with him either.

I finished roaming the base, looking in every room that I thought he could have even a remote possibility of being in, but in the end, I failed.

Either he was somewhere in this HQ but so concealed that I would never find him, or perhaps it wasn't him who had given the direct order after all, and it was one of his representatives here in Chicago. Maybe he was back in Canada, or in some other place. God knew.

I had no choice but to leave the IBSI headquarters and return to the city.

As I departed from the main entrance to the IBSI's compound, I found myself discovering street after street of horrors. The blown boundaries had caused the Bloodless to storm the city. I found myself wondering how they had even crossed the toxic river that was supposed to be acting as a natural second boundary. To my shock, I realized that bridges of long wooden slabs had been laid across the water at various intervals along the bank.

These people will stop at nothing.

Screams erupted as homes were raided, people being dragged outside and bitten before my very eyes.

I did what I could for a young man being attacked from just a few feet away from me—I slammed into the back of the offending Bloodless, causing him to lose balance, and knocked him away from the man. But it was clear that I had come too late. The man already had deep gash marks in his neck. And it would be only a matter of time before he turned too. There was hardly anything I could do to help these people. Not while I didn't have the antidote with me.

Hurry up! I found myself urging the others to return. Then, as I caught the sound of distant roaring, I realized that they already had. It was the roaring of dragons. During the extended period of time that I'd taken to search for Atticus in the IBSI's base, our group had arrived, even the slower-traveling firebreathers.

I spotted Xavier holding aloft two long, razor-sharp swords, beating back a group of three Bloodless who were encroaching on him. Then I spotted others: my sister, Caleb, Yuri, Kiev, and many more familiar faces mingling with the chaos and joining forces to fight the Bloodless back and prevent them from encroaching on the city even further.

"Hey, Rose," I called, hurrying toward my sister, who was focusing on not getting bitten by two Bloodless who were hurling themselves at her. "Where's Lawrence?" I asked.

She shrugged, not daring to take her eyes off the Bloodless, even as Caleb hurried to join her. "I don't know," she said. "Go look around."

I passed more friends and family—including Aiden and

Kailyn, as well as a large group of Hawks who were attempting to beat down a gang of ten Bloodless.

Our game plan now had to be to first get the Bloodless back on to the other side of the river, and then for the witches to put up another protective boundary. Only then could we think about moving to New York. We had no idea when exactly the IBSI would pull the trigger on the boundary there, but something told me that once they caught wind of our work here to regain control of the Bloodless, they would do it sooner rather than later, to overwhelm us. And then, after pulling the trigger on New York, there would likely be more.

We didn't have a second to lose.

But I still had unfinished business with Atticus. I found Lawrence stalking a parallel street, carrying two long blades.

"Lawrence," I called, relieved to find him, but hardly able to express it as I delivered the bad news. "I can't find your father anywhere in the base. Do you have any idea where else he could be? I checked everywhere I could possibly think of. I fear he might not be in Chicago after all."

Before he could answer, more Bloodless surrounded us—too many to hold a conversation in comfort. I grabbed Lawrence by the arms and then launched us upward into the air, setting us down on the roof of a nearby building.

Lawrence furrowed his brows. "Let me try calling his

phone."

Lawrence pulled out his phone that I had returned to him sometime back and dialed his father's number. He pressed the device to his ear, biting on his lower lip hard as it began to ring.

Ring, ring. Ring, ring.

No answer.

He tried again.

Still no luck.

I doubted either of us had actually expected Atticus to answer. Lawrence was not exactly on the best of terms with his father right now. I doubted whether Atticus would ever take another call from him again.

"Damn," Lawrence murmured, stowing the phone back into his pocket. "He could be anywhere."

Atticus

After giving the order, I decided that I wanted to watch everything play out. I took my private helicopter and flew it away from the IBSI's base, over the river, and landed it on one of the tallest buildings within Bloodless territory.

I watched as the Bloodless swarmed over the temporary bridges I had ordered be set up, and into the hapless residential quarters.

Could I honestly say that I didn't feel even the slightest twinge at doing this? No. There were families living in that area. I knew that. But I had to remind myself why I was doing any of this to begin with. Many more lives would be claimed and ruined in the future if we didn't make sacrifices now.

And besides, if it weren't for Lawrence and The Shadow League, none of this would even be required. There would have been minimal damage to people. But this was an important lesson that we had to teach not only The Shadow League, but the entire world. I had been monitoring the news reports that were spreading across the Internet like a virus, and I couldn't deny that many of the comments they were making about my organization stung. The vast majority of people already believed Lawrence, and the footage demonstrating the antidote in action. I still had no idea how they had actually managed to crack the antidotes and find all the right ingredients, since the first thing I'd done after Lawrence had betrayed me back in the lab was make sure the antidote ingredients were removed and transported somewhere where nobody would find them. Yes, they had managed to confiscate our stock of trees from Aviary, and it was possible that they had located the other plants from there, given that they were apparently now in alliance with the Hawks, but it still confused me as to how they could ever have gotten the blood that was required for the antidote.

But whatever the case, it was irrelevant now anyway. They had cracked the antidote and were apparently confident about creating enough of it to transform a significant number of Bloodless.

The screams and shouts piercing the night made my spine tingle.

The Shadow League had no clue. Absolutely no clue. I imagined they still thought that they could bring world peace by recruiting more of the supernaturals who were causing our problems in the first place. They probably still thought that they could trust them to turn into protectors. Well, now they had the perfect opportunity to test that theory, with the world as their audience.

After TSL's failure, the IBSI's position would only become stronger. Even if the world accused us of being duplicitous in our dealings, nobody could deny that we had kept people safe.

My phone was already exploding with phone calls. From representatives of the state, high government officials… even Lawrence's phone number popped up. Maybe TSL was already having second thoughts about their actions.

But I would make this lesson long and hard, so that when we finally retook control, TSL would have been shown to have failed so thoroughly and so publicly that there could never be any doubt about our leadership again.

The feeling of keeping the calls on hold was almost cathartic. Ignoring them. Causing them anxiety. No doubt if I didn't pick up soon, government officials would come flying over to look for me and beg me in person to resume our important work. I would not agree so easily. But when I did, I would have the upper hand to demand even more favorable terms for our organization.

The public themselves would also quickly change their minds about us. This constant slew of negative comments against the IBSI would quickly turn positive, out of desperation.

I waited a while longer before raising my phone to my ear and making the second most important call I would make that evening:

"Blow New York."

LAWRENCE

After I failed to get through to my father, Ben lowered us to the ground, where we continued assisting the others in fighting back the Bloodless. The witches and jinn were doing an effective job of stunning many at once, but these creatures were like rats. They scurried away and hid, out of reach from the spells, and it required an entire team to go poring through the streets in search of all the strays.

This task was much less nerve-racking for me than it was for the vampires among us. The Bloodless could still fatally wound me, but at least I was not at risk of turning into one of them.

Still, this task was made more difficult now that we knew that these were still real people who had the potential to be saved. Our reluctance to kill them significantly slowed our efforts to save the humans.

As the witches and jinn stunned Bloodless, and the rest of us attempted to herd them toward the magic-wielders, teams of vampires hurried to the rigid bodies and injected them with the antidote. Dr. Finnegan had managed to create a large amount by the time we'd returned. We stored a large stock in sturdy bags wrapped around the dragons' necks.

As I turned a corner, I was hit by a sudden blast of freezing cold air. A blue ice dragon named Lethe stood towering before me. He'd just blasted down shards of ice at a group of Bloodless in an attempt to drive them backward.

The fire dragons, so far, were being cautious about releasing their fire. I could see it was taking a lot of self-control to keep themselves in check, but releasing fire was far too dangerous when so many humans were still inside buildings, not to speak of the unnecessary loss of Bloodless lives.

I was just about to approach a trio of Bloodless I'd spotted running down an alleyway—attempt to use my knives to bully them toward the nearest witch—when I heard the sound of a helicopter slicing the air above me. My head panned upward. There was more than one. I expected them to be IBSI helicopters, immediately fearing that to add insult to injury, they were going to start bombing us… but I quickly realized that they did not belong to my father's organization.

They were navy blue, and smaller than any IBSI helicopter I had ever laid eyes on. Two of them were soaring toward the direction of the river, across it, and then over Bloodless territory.

Those were government helicopters. I was sure of it. I had seen this type before when government officials had come to visit my father in the past.

I felt the urge to follow them. I raced forward, using my supernatural speed to my full advantage. Dozens of Bloodless hurtled at me as I raced toward the river, and I was forced to slash out with my blades to beat them back before surging onward. I wouldn't have caused much harm—it was hard to cut off their limbs. The transformation did something to them that made dismembering them an arduous task.

My feet pounded over one of the wooden bridges, crossing the seething river and arriving on the other side. I continued to sprint, fearing that I would lose the helicopters, but I was able to keep up. They weren't traveling very fast, I realized. If anything, they seemed to be slowing down. Were they looking for something? Someone?

I followed them for miles across the city, doing all that I could to avoid bumping into Bloodless to delay my journey. Sometimes I had nothing but the aircrafts' noise to guide me as overhanging bridges or exceptionally tall buildings blocked my view. Then they stopped completely, hovering over what must have been one of the tallest skyscrapers in the area. They dipped down and appeared to land on its roof, the distant noise of their rotors dying down.

I stared at the smashed-up entrance of the dilapidated building. Entering such an enclosed space could be dangerous if there were Bloodless lurking inside. But I couldn't shake my curiosity. *What are government aircrafts doing on this side of the river, at a time like this?*

And so I hurried inside, keeping my weapons at the ready in case I needed to defend myself. The elevators were of course out of order, so I was forced to take the winding stairwell. Climbing it wasn't a fraction of the task it would've been had I still been a regular human. Fortunately, I met no Bloodless on the way. I scaled the steps swiftly, until I reached the top.

I crept to a grimy window that looked out onto the flat roof. Keeping close to the wall to avoid being seen, I peered out. There were three helicopters—the two blue ones that I had seen land, but also a third one… a black IBSI aircraft. Nearby stood two men. My breath hitched as I realized that one of them was my father, standing tall in a long gray trenchcoat, and the second one was a short man with slicked-back white hair wearing a beige overcoat. I didn't recognize him, but he must've descended from one of the government helicopters. I moved closer to the door and pressed my ear against the crack, straining to hear what they were saying.

"Ask for what you will," the official was saying, "But you've got to begin work to reinstate the barriers."

My father slipped his hands into his deep pockets and kicked around some gravel. His eyes passed over the dark city surrounding them.

"I wonder if perhaps you would be better served by TSL," he said calmly. "Have you not considered that they might indeed provide superior protection, as they are promising?"

"Atticus," the official said, his voice tightening. "We don't have time. You have heard our order."

My father dallied a little longer—I could see that a part of him was enjoying keeping the old man on eggshells. *Keeping the world on eggshells.*

"You know that we can fix this situation swiftly," he replied. "But in return I'm going to ask for measures to ensure that TSL cannot cause damage to our organization again."

The old man's brows rose, urging my father to go on.

"I need you to shut down everything. Put a hold on every

news station. Call for a temporary closure of every major online news portal. I need there to be less noise, and I need full control."

The man barely hesitated. "Understood. But for how long?"

"Until I tell you to allow them to resurface," my father replied dryly.

"It will be done," the man said. "What is your time estimate to fix this?"

My father ran a tongue over his lower lip. "I'll keep you updated," was all that he responded.

The men shook hands, and then the two of them retreated to their respective helicopters—the official into one of the blue ones, my father climbing into the black one, which, I guessed, he had piloted here on his own.

As the doors of the aircrafts began to close, I was faced with a dilemma. I was tempted to launch after my father— not allow him to get away—but something told me that that would only cause me to wind up getting trapped in the IBSI's base again, and this time, I doubted I would ever reemerge. Especially since I didn't know that my father's chopper was empty; he could have armed men in there who could help overpower me, for all I knew.

Between the two, I figured that I would have a better chance of achieving something productive with the official.

My father's chopper rose into the air before the blue ones. It swept away from the roof and began soaring back toward the IBSI's headquarters. The government helicopters were slower, perhaps engaging in some discussion before their rotors sped up and they began to levitate off the ground.

I had to hurry.

Gripping the handle of the metal door, I tried to push it open. It was locked. Not having the patience to break through it, I opted for the easier target—the window. Taking a few steps back, I sent myself crashing through it, managing to land on my feet on the other side. As the distance increased between the ground and the helicopters' skids, I darted toward the one I knew the old man was riding in and grabbed hold of the metal landing gear.

If the passengers noticed a sudden jolt, they didn't show it. The helicopter continued rising, steadily, and then began to soar in the opposite direction of the IBSI's HQ, a sheer drop of hundreds of feet suddenly appearing beneath me. I kept my gaze firmly upward on the aircraft's underbelly, even as my palms felt sweaty against the metal. Swallowing hard, I glanced upward toward the closed door. Finding my balance on the skids, I pulled myself up into a standing position, even as I reached up and rapped loudly against the metal.

There was a beat, and then the door slid open. I slipped a

hand through the crack and forced it open wider before thrusting myself upward and landing on the floor of the aircraft. Gasps of men swept around me, including from the white-haired man.

I shot to my feet as several guards around me clutched their guns.

I fixed my gaze on the old man's. "You recognize me, don't you?" I said steadily.

"How could we not?" he managed.

"I need you to discard everything that my father just told you," I told him sternly. Somehow, I had to keep the major news portals open. The government operated all the main news channels—both online and offline—and if they were shut down, it would cause confusion and panic among people, and it would hamper the speed at which the truth was currently being spread to the public.

"I am with TSL," I said. "You *need* to give us a chance to fix this. If you give back full control to the IBSI so easily, then nothing will ever have a hope of changing. You watched my broadcast, didn't you?"

The man nodded, as did every other man in the chopper. I couldn't help but notice that their grip around their guns had loosened a touch.

"Then you're fully aware of how the IBSI has been deceiving you and the world. You are desperate right now.

But that's exactly where the IBSI wants you—in a place of blind need and helplessness. If you don't give TSL a chance, then nothing ever has a chance of changing, and the IBSI will only grow more and more corrupt."

The man's brows knotted. "Have *you* not heard what's been going on?" he said. "Have you not *seen?* We are in a state of emergency! Lives are being—"

"I know," I said heavily. "I know. I've just come from the epicenter of the Bloodless infestation in Chicago. If you glance down over the city, on the other side of the river, you will see members of TSL already there combating the situation. Albeit not as effectively as we would like to yet… We need more time to prove to you and the world that the IBSI are no longer needed."

The man rubbed his temples, looking uncertainly to each of his colleagues. "Time is exactly what we don't have, Mr. Conway."

"Then buy some," I said, glaring at him. "Even if it's a few hours. *Buy some.*"

I knew that if the government hesitated in shutting down the news portals, my father, too, wouldn't hesitate to wreak more havoc. It was vital that we stop them from regaining full control while keeping the news channels open, because if they were allowed to reassert their boundaries, once all the news feeds did flow freely again, the IBSI would only be considered even more of a necessity than they'd been before. Even though we had broadcast their corruption and downright inhumanity, all of it would get swept under the carpet in light of the threat of the Bloodless flooding their residential cities and suburbs. Everybody would be convinced once and for all that it was not possible to live without the IBSI, even if they wished that they could. There would be no more opening for TSL in the public's minds after such a horrific and widespread failure. Everybody would be desperate for the boundaries to never fall again, regardless of what it meant giving up in return for their safety. There would be no room left for morals, truth, or dignity to play a part in anything.

This was exactly my father's plan. I could practically see the wheels turning in his head as I imagined him flying back toward base.

I had to stall the news channels going down, and I had to get these people to give TSL a chance. A real chance—a chance that they should've been given decades ago.

When the man hesitated, I pressed, my eyes boring into him, "Please, even a few hours."

I feared that hours wouldn't be enough, but it was better than the government pulling the plug on the news channels now.

I breathed out in relief as the man replied in a cracking

voice, "I need to make some calls."

With that, he turned and strode into the cockpit, closing the door firmly behind him.

I looked to the men surrounding me, and their guns. "You can lower them," I informed them. "I promise you that I'm not here for trouble. I, and all of TSL… we are on your side, despite what the IBSI might have led you to believe about us. We're not just meddlesome rebels." It both struck and warmed me as I realized how natural it felt to me to refer to the TSL as *we*. The Shade and its people had been a part of my life for such a short span of time and yet I felt more at home on that island with them than I'd ever felt anywhere else in my life.

I sat down in an empty seat, clasping my hands together, elbows resting on my knees. The wait was excruciating. I couldn't hear what was being said because the door to the pilot's compartment was thick and bulletproof—apparently soundproof too.

Finally, the man emerged. His forehead was wrinkled with worry as he laid his eyes on me and said, "We will delay granting your father's request by two hours. You had better show us what you're capable of within that time, because I can assure you that you won't be given another chance if you fail."

As relieved as I was, I was also terrified. I gazed out of the window over the residential area that we were beginning to cross. I could make out the imposing forms of the dragons, and the smaller forms of the rest of TSL still darting about the streets.

Derek… you had better hurry the heck up.

GRACE

Orlando, Field and his friends, my mother and I were sitting in Orlando's bedroom, gaping at the screen of my open laptop. Field was in a daze, as were his companions; the Bloodless seemed a fairly new species to them, which was ironic considering their blood was one of the keys to combating them.

The screen displayed a scene of utter desolation, a scene that belonged in my darkest nightmares of the time that Orlando and I had spent in Bloodless Chicago. It was a time that I'd been trying to purge from my brain, but watching the reporters stream footage from New York City brought it all flooding back. My skin broke out in goosebumps.

Waves of Bloodless washed through the city, spilling into homes and digging their fangs into all they passed. Men, women, families, none were spared.

"Oh, God," I choked. "What is happening? Where are our people?"

My question was answered as we switched to a broadcast that was covering Chicago. Here, at least, was a more hopeful scene. I spotted a few of our witches in the clips as they cast freezing spells upon swathes of the monsters. Then more of our army would hurry over to administer injections of antidote. They appeared to be making more progress than I'd expected.

But this was only one city. New York was still a complete mess.

I groaned. "What's going to—?"

"Hey, there's your dad," my mother said, excitement lighting up her worried voice. Yes. There he was. His dark hair rippling in the night breeze, he was in a semi-subtle state, his feet on the ground. He was luring a group of Bloodless toward a group of jinn at the end of his street. They stunned the monsters before they stooped over them with the antidote.

"We need more people out there," I said, gripping the sheets of my bed. "We need *tons* more people." I wished I could help in even some small, indirect way. It was endlessly frustrating sitting here helpless in bed.

And when was the next city going to fall? Would the IBSI keep withdrawing? What if they withdrew from everywhere?

Before I could sink deeper into worry about how far the IBSI was willing to go to make their point, there was a knock at our door.

It was Shayla. I would've leapt from the bed in surprise to greet her if I had been strong enough.

But she hardly had eyes for me, or for my mother. Her focus went straight to Orlando. "Honey," she said, "Come with me."

Orlando looked utterly confused as he stared back at the witch. He glanced at me, but I shared his confusion. Then he slipped himself off the bed, into a wheelchair—he, like me, was still shaky after taking the antidote—and wheeled out of the room after the witch.

My mom helped me into my own chair and we hurried after him. The witch led us to the end of the corridor before stopping outside a door. Gripping the handle, she pushed it open. Orlando, entering first, gasped. As my mother and I arrived inside next to him, I realized why. My jaw dropped.

Lying on the bed, bald, emaciated and pale, was his sister Maura.

Orlando broke down. His hands slipped on the wheels of

his chair in his urgency to push himself to her.

"Orlando!" Maura rasped, apparently too weak to raise herself to hug him. Shayla helped him perch on the edge of the bed so he could take his sister in his arms and hold her. His back began to heave as he wept against her.

Shayla, my mom and I backed out of the room, giving the siblings some privacy.

"How on earth did you find her?" I asked the witch.

"I didn't," Shayla replied. "Corrine and Ben returned with her and two other turned humans. They told me to bring the trio back to The Shade. We've been back for a while, actually. It only just occurred to me how familiar the girl was… It struck me that she looked like Orlando, and then I remembered Orlando's missing sister. She was in and out of consciousness but as soon as I mentioned her brother's name she woke right up."

A smile spread across my face, tears moistening the corners of my eyes. I might not be able to give Orlando the affection he wanted—and probably deserved—from me, but at least he'd found his sister. At least Maura was back. And cured now. They both were cured. No longer watching the hours go by, wondering when their last would come.

And I hope, if and when all this is over, he'll find the spark he seeks in me in some other Shade girl's eyes.

BEⅡ

As much progress as we were beginning to make in Chicago, we were also suffering major setbacks— something that the recently-arrived helicopters filled with press reporters flashing lights and cameras were capturing every minute of. These Bloodless were pesky creatures. Just when we thought we had cleared an area and we moved on to the next, more would spring out from corners. We even had a fiasco where a group of missed Bloodless dug into a pile of turning ones we had separated, which overwhelmed the turning and caused them to start returning to their prior monstrous forms.

The reporters were distracting with all the noise they brought with them—there was enough noise being created by our team as we tried to coordinate our efforts—but I knew that their presence was important.

This was TSL's time to prove itself. And although we had barely even started yet, we had to make a good impression.

It worried me, however, that we were running out of antidote. I sent Safi back to The Shade to get some more—hoping that Dr. Finnegan and her assistants would have had time by now to create a vat more of the stuff. She had already discovered how to make the ingredients—particularly the Hawk boys' blood—stretch; now we needed to mass-produce the antidote as quickly as possible.

As I spotted yet another pocket of undiscovered Bloodless clambering up the side of the building, I went hurrying after them. *Come here, you buggers.* But as I reached the roof, I was distracted by a particularly low-hanging helicopter. A blue helicopter. It touched down on the building directly opposite me, and a man stepped out. A man whom I quickly realized was Lawrence. He exchanged a few words with whoever was in the belly of the aircraft before it lifted back up into the air.

"Hey, Lawrence!" I yelled, even as I lost sight of the Bloodless. I'd track them down again soon enough. I was too confused by Lawrence's sudden appearance. I hadn't even known that he'd been absent; I'd thought he might have been helping out in a different street.

I soared over and landed in front of him. His lips were pursed, a storm of worry behind his brown eyes.

"What's going on? Where have you been?"

"We have two hours," he said hoarsely.

"What?"

As he recounted to me the meeting that had taken place between his father and a government official—whom I suspected might have been our old contact, Fowler—I understood why Lawrence was looking so ashen.

Two hours was no time at all. But it was what we'd been given, and as Lawrence said, it was better than nothing at all.

"I know where my father is," he said, clutching my shoulder. "He's headed back to the IBSI's base. He'll be waiting for the official to make good on his word before resuming instructions to his men. My guess is that he'll be in his office. If he realizes that the official has stalled in shutting down the news channels, he might cause destruction in yet another city out of frustration. I suggest you and maybe another fae go to him now and try to isolate him, if only to stop him from ordering more chaos. At least for the next two hours."

I cast my gaze toward the direction of the IBSI's base and nodded. "All right," I murmured. "I'll pay your father another visit."

Atticus

I sighed as I took a seat in my office chair and flipped open my laptop. As I surfed the web, it was clear that the old man had not yet fulfilled his end of the deal. I drummed my fingers on the table surface.

He should've given the order as soon as he climbed back into the helicopter, as he had mentioned that he would…

My hand reached into my pocket. I pulled out my phone and set it down in front of me, my fingers turning it in circles.

I realized that I should've set a time limit in our negotiation, otherwise they could dawdle. I composed a text message, stating that I needed to see some progress on their end of the deal within the next half hour, or I might reconsider my promise.

If they failed for whatever reason to uphold their part of our agreement, I would let down the borders of Los Angeles next. Then, perhaps, Washington. I wanted them to realize just how dependent on us they were. The world had taken us for granted all these years, assuming that we would always be there to serve and protect them. Hence the public believed they could get away with insulting us, calling us cheats and frauds.

My actions would soon clear up those insults, and no doubt the government would be quick to fulfill their promises.

I stared at my phone screen in wait for their reply. *Come on, Fowler. What are you playing at?*

A response came thirteen minutes later. *Thirteen* minutes. *"We are working on it."*

Something strange was going on. Prior to our meeting, Fowler had been harassing me with messages every other minute, asking me what the heck was going on and requesting an urgent meeting. It was strange that he should become so lax.

My nostrils flared as I breathed in. *Something isn't right.*

I waited another five minutes before checking the web

again. All of the portals Fowler had promised would be suspended were still active. They were buzzing and alive as ever. I switched on my television. Every single news channel here was also blaring full blast—each of them covering the situation with the Bloodless and... I squinted as I caught sight of familiar faces among the ravaged Chicago streets. TSL. Their members were here already, attempting to pick up the pieces.

I rose to my feet and began tensely pacing up and down. I would wait ten more minutes before making the call to LA. Ten. More. Minutes. And then I would verify whose loyalties lay where.

I watched the minutes go by tensely. When there was no sign of any improvement after twelve minutes, I'd had enough.

I dialed the number of my commander-in-chief in LA and pressed the speaker to my ear. But I barely heard the second ring. A heavy book came hurtling toward me from the other side of the room. It crashed into my hand, its sharp edge grazing the side of my cheek and causing the phone to clatter to the floor.

My eyes shot to the other side of the room — where the book had hurtled from — to find two phantom-like creatures drifting toward me. I recognized one enough to know his name. Benjamin Novak. TSL's cofounder. And then there was a female fae with curly blonde hair.

Before I could draw my gun, the fae had hurtled toward me with extreme speed. His hands clamped around my throat, and we went zooming backward, my back hitting the glass bookshelves behind me and causing them to topple to the floor.

"Smash the camera, Kailyn," Benjamin hissed over his shoulder to the woman. I strained to see the woman rising up toward the CCTV camera positioned in one corner of the ceiling. She broke the lens with a book.

Benjamin wrestled with me on the ground. He managed to flip me over on my stomach before gripping my arms from behind and pinning me in a firm hold.

Damn fae. They and jinn were two creatures who had still managed to evade our security measures to this day.

He pressed his weight down on me, squashing the side of my face against the floor.

"What were you just planning to do?" he asked, his voice a hiss in my ear.

"Release our boundaries in LA," I spat back. "What's it to you what we do or do not do anymore? You're so confident that you can solve this situation on your own."

His grip around my wrists tightened.

"Make sure his phone is dead," Benjamin hissed to the woman.

She did so, before chucking my phone in the trash can. The sight made me wince. My phone was, arguably, the most valuable possession I owned. But it wasn't irreplaceable— just like I wasn't.

"May I ask what you hope to accomplish by taking me prisoner?" I asked them calmly. "You won't stop anything. As I'm sure I mentioned to you before, my disappearance won't make an awful lot of difference to the IBSI. I have people and measures in place to ensure that it endures long, long after I pass. If anything, your holding me here will quicken the release of the third city."

Benjamin didn't answer, though I sensed my words had knocked his confidence. His grip loosened just a touch—not enough to give me leeway to squirm out, but enough for me to be able to breathe more freely.

"Well?" I prompted.

That was the good thing about serving a cause you believed in. It made you fearless. I wasn't afraid of death, or of pain, while pursuing the path I deemed right. I would rather die in glory than live in compromise. And there were others like me, too. Others I had personally hand-picked and trained over the years, who shared my vision. I trusted they would continue where I left off, even if something did happen to me. Take, for example, Bernard in LA. After receiving my call and being cut off, he would suspect something. He was following the news and the developments with Fowler; I had been keeping him informed. He would have the sense to pull the trigger on LA soon enough, and then other cities, if I still hadn't managed to regain control over myself and a phone by that time.

"You won't get away with this, Atticus." Benjamin's low voice came in my ear. "I assure you, neither you nor any of your men will get away with this. We *will* take your place, and you will fade into insignificance… It's only a matter of time."

Empty threats by a desperate man. Hardly words I was going to take seriously. And yet, as Benjamin raised me from the floor and made me stand on my feet, still gripping me and preventing me from reaching for a weapon, I sensed a determination in him that made me think twice. His confidence unsettled me. He seemed to fully believe that his words were no joke, even in the face of overwhelming destruction—destruction which, in all truth, even we would have a tough time setting right again.

What is he thinking?

Does he truly believe The Shadow League could replace the IBSI?

BEN

I had grown tired of Atticus's taunts, as well as wrestling him to keep him constrained. I removed Atticus's shirt and bound it tightly around his wrists, to serve as makeshift handcuffs. I confiscated any weapons he had on his person and threw them to Kailyn, who placed them on a shelf on the opposite end of the room—except for his gun, which she held aimed at Atticus.

I sat him down in his office chair and approached his laptop.

Only days ago, my first instinct at the sight of his open laptop would be to search it for the Bloodless antidote. It was a relief to have finally cracked that mystery. Now, I pulled up his web browser to see that he had been searching the internet—for news channels that were still showing no signs of closing down. I glanced at the television opposite us. It was displaying coverage of TSL's activities in Chicago. As more footage flashed of New York, my stomach churned. We had barely scratched the surface of the destruction. And we had only two hours before the IBSI got their way, and everyone as good as accepted that they and their methods—however backhanded and duplicitous—were the only solution to Earth's problems.

Kailyn kept the television on channels displaying the scene in Chicago. The cameramen seemed particularly interested in following our people, which was good. They showed our method of dealing with the Bloodless—cure rather than kill, at least in all possible cases. If we were the IBSI, we would have done something rash like bomb the area, regardless of whatever innocent humans still remained hiding in their homes from the Bloodless.

Atticus became unexpectedly quiet. I glanced back at him, frowning and wondering what was going through his head.

I didn't know how long we'd be able to keep him locked up in here before security personnel figured out that something was odd—probably noticing the camera in Atticus' office had gone blank. I moved instinctively to the door and made sure it was closed firmly.

We had less than two hours to camp out in here, but that was a long time to keep a hostage like Atticus cooped up.

I pushed his chair closer to the television so that I myself could be closer to it without constantly checking on him over my shoulder.

Once we hit the one-hour mark, it was hard to keep hoping. Even in spite of our diligence, our small group in Chicago was still struggling to get a handle on the Bloodless. The area was just so massive, making the dozens of streets we had managed to clear seem insignificant. Many Bloodless had simply migrated to other parts of the ravaged city, and there were still countless families trapped in their homes or being preyed upon at this very moment by the monsters.

By now, we had brought along every single person from The Shade capable of helping us with this mission, and yet we desperately needed more people.

The dragons would be tempted to take a similar approach to that of the IBSI—release storms of fire and burn out the monsters. But we could not. We had to do this right, every step of the way, if we wanted to stand a chance of distinguishing ourselves from the IBSI and striking a chord in the hearts of the public. They needed to *want* us to rise to authority, rather than simply accepting us because they had no other choice, as was the case with the IBSI's reign for the past few decades.

Then came the announcement that I had feared would come—Los Angeles had fallen. Atticus had not been bluffing when he said that his colleague was ready to pull the trigger. Now we had three cities to contend with. I found it hard to believe that the government would be able to stall granting Atticus's wish much longer, though all channels still remained active. It seemed that the authorities really were desperate for an alternative to the IBSI.

The second hour came upon us and began to pass at a frighteningly fast pace.

The minutes were punctuated by flashes of nightmares from the cities. Even the channel that had been focusing on Chicago began to switch to the newly invaded LA. It was hard to keep watching, witnessing so starkly just how outnumbered we were.

"He's not going to arrive in time," Kailyn whispered, apparently forgetting that Atticus was still present with us. I gritted my teeth. I did not want to give him the satisfaction of my response, or for him to guess whom, exactly, Kailyn had meant by "he".

A loud ringing shrilled through Atticus's office, snapping our attention to the door. The ringing was Atticus's front doorbell. Some concerned colleagues, no doubt, had come to see if he was all right.

"You see," Atticus said calmly, his cold eyes traveling from the office door to Kailyn and me, "I suspected that all of this was out of your league, excuse the pun. Best to leave these matters to us in the future—not that you will have any choice anyway."

The ringing became more intense, more impatient, and turned to loud banging and crashing against the front door. The final minutes passed more rapidly than ever. I couldn't help but entertain the doubt that perhaps Atticus was right.

We've missed the deadline, as Lawrence and I feared we would.

My father has not managed to save the day.

LAWRENCE

I fumbled in my pocket for the phone I'd requested from the government official before leaving the aircraft. Two hours were up, but I had to at least attempt to wrangle some more time. We were making some progress—that much had been broadcast to the world by the reporters hovering over the scene. I was sure that the authorities were watching every moment of it. But we had failed to make the impact that was required to actually solve this problem. We hadn't gotten anywhere close.

I dialed the official's number. He picked up after a few rings. "It's Lawrence," I said, yelling into the phone beneath the blare of the rotors above me. "Please, give us some more time. You can see what we're capable of—we're just waiting for—"

"I'm sorry," he replied sharply. "We were overly generous with two hours. You've had your chance to shine. Now we must hand everything back to the IBSI. We are in the process of carrying out your father's request."

"No!" I shouted, my right hand gripping the phone so tightly it felt that it might crack beneath the pressure. "Please, listen to me!"

"I'm sorry, Mr. Conway. I cannot speak with you anymore."

With that, the phone hung up.

Clenching my fists together, I brought them smashing against the wall of a nearby building. *Dammit!*

Given that Ben had not returned from the base, I could only assume that he had managed to find my father and was holding him captive. But that did not matter now. His commanders would take over issuing orders if he was still not able to.

I wasn't sure what was going to happen next, but as the press helicopters began to withdraw from the scene, I knew that I had to warn everyone. With the IBSI back in the saddle, it was dangerous for us to be here any longer. They would've witnessed our work, and something told me that this area was going to be their first, most vicious target.

I gazed around at the heaps of recovering humans we had managed to gather. I feared that all of them were at risk now. All of them.

I yelled to TSL members as I raced down the streets. "The IBSI are going to begin closing in! We need to get everyone we saved out of here while we can. And then, if we're able to, come back for the rest."

Somehow, I doubted the likelihood of the latter once the IBSI sank their claws into this land. I feared what it would become. The lengths they would go to in an effort to "restore order".

I stopped short in front of Corrine. She had whirled around to look at me, hands on hips, beads of sweat lining her forehead. "We can't retreat," she said, looking at me as though I'd gone mad.

Other TSL members who were not immediately occupied with the Bloodless also began to surround me. "Maybe not *us*," I said. I shouldn't have been surprised that the people of The Shade were expecting to stay to the bitter end. "But the humans we've turned—we must get them out of here. Back to The Shade, *anywhere* but here."

Corrine swallowed, and turned to our jinn and witches. "Okay," she called to them, "Start working on transporting humans, and turning humans, back to The Shade … But the rest of us must stay. We can't let the IBSI think we can be defeated so easily."

I admired the bravery of the witch, and all the other men and women I'd been fighting alongside for the past several hours. I just hoped that we were ready for this. Because once the IBSI hit, they would be taking no prisoners.

LAWRENCE

The witches and jinn cooperated to transport the piles of humans and turning-humans back to the island, and returned swiftly. My eyes kept flitting up to the sky, even as we continued to search the city for survivors. I was expecting a cloud of black helicopters to descend on us from the direction of the base at any moment. For a storm of mutants to come rushing our way.

The mutants came first.

Their arrival announced by a painful symphony of screeches, hundreds of them became visible in the murky sky.

The mutants were like bloodhounds for Bloodless. I should know. I'd witnessed them being trained on several occasions.

The witches and jinn hurried to transfer the final batch of humans, while the rest of us rushed together in a huddle before the mutants reached us. We gathered with the dragons, who were carrying the bulk of our weapons. I slid my swords into the sheaths on either side of my belt before picking up a machine gun. Then everyone quickly mounted the dragons.

I opted for Lethe, the only ice dragon among us, since he was close to me. I climbed onto his sleek blue-scaled back and settled myself behind his neck, even as his heavy wings spread and beat. We lifted into the sky along with the fire dragons. I double-checked the gun was loaded and fired to verify that it was all in order. Then my eyes set straight ahead, on the army of mutants. They were almost upon us now, and I could make out IBSI members riding on their backs, dressed in dark heat-resistant clothing and equipped with heavy firearms.

If they had been after the Bloodless alone, there would've been no need for so many humans among the mutants. The mutants were well trained to go sniffing for Bloodless and eradicating them. No. It was clear that their first priority was to come after us.

Our dragons were larger and more powerful than the mutants, but the mutants grossly outnumbered them. They were also tough and sturdy, with high pain tolerance levels. They didn't have natural armor as thick as the dragons' though.

The fire dragons unleashed billows of flames in anticipation, creating a massive wall of fire in front of us. Of course, in a sense, having so many humans among them worked to our advantage. Although the humans wore protection, the mutants could not be quite so ruthless in their attack as they would have been without their masters.

I was not sure exactly what role Lethe was going to play in all of this. He was an ice dragon. But as the fire dragons continued to unleash their fire—fierce enough to have blazed up from Hell itself—Lethe flew upward with me, as if to avoid it.

"You can't take the heat well?" I commented.

"No," he said, his voice tight. "I cannot."

This was going to be a battle he'd need to be careful in, then. At least he could fly around and give me a vantage point.

The fire dragons maintained their wall of fire, but as the mutants closed the final distance, they began flying around it, over it and beneath it. Then the hunters began firing bullets. I cursed as I gazed down at our group. The witches and jinn hadn't returned yet. They'd better hurry up!

We had brought armor with us from The Shade in anticipation, which many had donned, but that didn't stop me from being afraid that we might suffer some fallen soldiers, especially the vampires. The hunters wouldn't have arrived without their special UV-ray guns.

"Careful, guys!" I roared down, my stomach clenching with nervousness.

The dragons swirled and switched directions suddenly, sending fire shooting in all directions, which only caused poor Lethe to fly higher in the sky. I began firing down bullets at hunters. Although they wore protection, they still had vulnerabilities. Just as even our dragons did. I managed to topple three hunters from the initial surge, sending them tumbling to the ground, their mutants left abandoned.

"Can you fly a bit higher still?" I asked Lethe.

He was happy to oblige. He soared upward over what was becoming an increasingly difficult scene to watch. So much smoke was emanating from the flames and firearms— including grenades, which our army were beginning to chuck— it became a scorching blur of fire and chaos.

I looked eastward to see a group of helicopters hovering in the air. Press reporters. Some stray ones hadn't abandoned us yet. Perhaps they were even recording, though now that the IBSI had come back into power, there was no way they'd be allowed to broadcast that. At least not yet.

I tried to use my height and the smoky atmosphere to my advantage, taking out several more hunters from above. The machine gun rattled in my hands, sending tremors rolling up my arms and through my body. I was barely even registering that I was killing people. Men and women, probably most around my age. In this battle, it was kill or be killed. They had chosen their side, and I'd chosen mine.

My grip tightened around my gun. It was my father and all the other IBSI puppeteers who should be out here on the front line. Not these brainwashed young men and women.

That was what I respected about TSL. They weren't leaders watching from ivory towers. They were on the ground as foot soldiers, always the first into battle. They did whatever was required. Though perhaps I couldn't fault my father too severely for that. He was a tough man, and getting his hands dirty certainly wasn't beneath him, given how much he believed in his cause. Maybe we would see him yet, if Ben ever let him go.

As I continued raining down bullets on the army, I sprayed both mutants and hunters, attempting to weaken as much of their cavalry as possible.

Six hunters banded together and began rising with their mutants, fed up with the nuisance I was causing. They rose swiftly above the smoke.

I expected Lethe to use his supernatural speed and strength to surge upward, but instead, he drew in a deep breath and breathed out a storm of ice shards.

The mutants screeched at the unexpected winter storm. The hunters looked shocked too. Either they didn't know Lethe was an ice dragon, or they'd never come across one before. The mutants staggered in the air, falling backward as the shards dug into their bodies. Lethe's powerful breath battered the humans, although they tried to duck behind the mutants' heads for protection.

The mutants retreated a dozen feet, while Lethe remained on the offense. He breathed down more ice, and more, until the mutants had dropped back down into the heat of the battle.

I patted the back of the dragon's neck with one hand. "Good going."

My feeling of accomplishment didn't last long. The hunters we'd beaten down gathered more mutants—there must have been twenty in total—and came flying at us again.

Anticipating Lethe's ice, they began to breathe out flames in advance, so that by the time they reached within ten feet of us they had created a substantial sea of flames above them as protection. This proved to be problematic for Lethe. He attempted to shoot down more ice, but the fire, so close to him, appeared to be weakening him. He managed only a small gust before he retreated higher into the sky. Now, it seemed that we had no choice but to switch to defense. Slotting my feet firmly into the gaps of Lethe's scales, I twisted around and leaned my back against his neck so that I could rain down bullets. I shot them down blindly though, due to the smoke the flames were creating. My eyes stung and watered, blurring my vision further.

Lethe climbed higher to reach clean air. Clutching his scales with one hand, I rose to my feet while leaning against his neck for a better view. The vicious creatures were still chasing after us. We had aggravated them and their owners, and they weren't going to let us off easily.

They blazed more fire toward us, and to my horror, I realized that Lethe was beginning to slow down.

"What's going on?" I called into his right ear. "You need to keep going!"

Lethe at his full speed was faster than the mutants, but they were not to be underestimated. They still possessed supernatural speed, and they were small and agile, able to switch directions faster than a dragon. Lethe's breathing was becoming labored.

"I know," he wheezed.

"It's the heat?" I shouted over the screeching of the mutants.

He grunted.

The prolonged exposure to heat. Even now, the mutants were continuing to breathe fire, and we could feel it from a distance.

"Okay," I said, trying to maintain my calm. "We've got to shake them off." I glanced at them over my shoulder. Clenching my teeth, I doused them with more bullets.

The hunters shot back through the flames this time, and I was forced to duck down, shield myself behind Lethe's scales to avoid being hit.

"Lethe, listen to me," I said. His pace was continuing to lag. "You need to take a sharp dive, when I say." I repositioned myself on his back, making sure that I was holding on tight enough. "Three. Two. One. Dive!"

He dove abruptly, and diagonally, missing the mutants' flames. The combination of gravity and Lethe continuing to beat his wings allowed us to move faster, even if our direction was back down to the ground. I was too preoccupied with holding on to check behind me, but I could hear the mutants had also changed direction and were following us. Lethe wasn't the only one for whom gravity worked as an advantage. I felt the dragon's body vibrate as he let out an anguished groan.

I felt a sudden surge of heat, so close to me, it practically scorched my back.

I twisted my neck. *Damn.* One of the mutants had

reached closer than I'd imagined. His fire had scorched Lethe's tail. In our freefall, I couldn't maintain enough balance to hold on to Lethe's back and shoot at the same time.

I was running out of ideas. And we had almost reached the ground. At least we had swerved around the brunt of the battle, where the air was cooler. But it wouldn't remain cool for long with these mutants on our literal tail.

Lethe grunted again. As I looked back this time, I caught sight of the fire climbing up his tail. His flight became unsteady. We careened toward the roof of a skyscraper.

"No!" I yelled into his ear. "You've got to keep flying! Don't touch down!" They would scorch the two of us alive.

The rest of the mutants caught up. And although Lethe valiantly continued his attempts to remain aloft, it seemed as though with each beat of his wings he grew weaker. His scales were strong against many things, but not heat.

One more blaze of fire, and I was sure that he would fall. As the mutants screeched together, their chests sucking in, I braced myself for a fatal tsunami of fire.

But instead, a violent gust of wind rushed over our heads. It had come from the opposite direction of the mutants. Although Lethe and I were not in its direct path to receive the brunt of it, it caused him to stagger in the air. And as for the mutants who were in its direct path, they were sucked backward, away from us, as if being pulled by a vacuum cleaner.

Lethe landed on the ground with a shudder. His legs collapsed beneath him. I slid off his back even as I tried to see where the magical wind had come from. Then I spotted Corrine, in the sky, along with four other jinn. Thank God, they had returned from their final transfer of the humans to The Shade. They must have spotted Lethe and I zooming down from the sky like a meteor.

The jinn's focus remained on the mutants. They hurtled after them while Corrine descended to us. Her eyes bulged with concern.

"Lethe?" she said, touching him on the snout. "Are you okay?"

Lethe groaned.

I stood next to her to get a better look at the ice dragon's face, and then I cast my eyes over the rest of his body. Corrine moved to examine his tail. It was blistering. She ran her palms down the length of it and muttered something beneath her breath. Lethe flinched and twitched, shifting his body across the ground away from her, but she maintained her grip.

Then the ice dragon relaxed.

"Feel any better?" Corrine asked him.

"Weak," he mumbled, but at least he was slowly rising to

his feet now. He raised his wings, testing them.

"I think we should take you back to The Shade," Corrine said, biting her lip.

To my surprise, Lethe shook his head. "I'll stay around the borders of the battle and be careful not to get into such trouble again."

Lethe lowered his head, apparently expecting me to climb onto his back again. But I needed to be more involved in this battle than Lethe could be. A part of me felt responsible for the IBSI's mess. It was, after all, my father at the root of it all. This was my battle, possibly more than anyone else's. *Mine, and my mother's.*

"You do what you need to," I told the dragon. "Don't worry about me anymore. Just keep safe."

He nodded before launching into the sky again. His flight was shaky at first, but I suspected that he would not go far. Probably find a nearby skyscraper to perch on until he regained his strength.

I looked at Corrine, who was gazing up at the sky in the direction where the jinn had herded the mutants. I could hear the sounds of the battle, the thick of which was taking place about twenty streets away. The gunshots. The shouts. More screeching of mutants.

"I'm going to return to the others," Corrine said, rolling up her sleeves. "What's your plan?"

I wanted to venture through the streets a bit before returning to the sky. I might be able to take out a hunter or two in the process.

"Don't let me hold you back," I told her.

"All right." She lifted into the air, and I was about to go darting down a street to my left when a ball of fiery red zoomed past me. Its heat singed my skin as it hurtled in the direction of Corrine, whose back was turned. I barely had a chance to yell out before it hit her square in the lower back.

She let out a strangled gasp. And then she was falling. Adrenaline exploding in my veins, I jolted forward in an attempt to catch her, but I never got the chance. Another blur whooshed past me: a blur of brown. It was a woman, hurtling through the sky. A woman with limp blonde hair, wearing a long brown dress. She flew to catch Corrine in her arms. She was another witch.

"Loira!" Corrine gasped, even as she began to fight her off.

Whatever spell Loira had thrown at Corrine had weakened her, however. Her attempts to break free from her grip were feeble.

"What are you—?" Corrine demanded, anger, and undertones of pain, coursing through her voice.

Before she could finish her question Loira sent her hurtling toward the side of a building. Corrine crashed through the glass and disappeared from my view. My heart was in my throat as Loira zoomed after her.

What is that witch doing? Where did she come from? I had never seen her before, and she certainly wasn't a witch of The Shade.

There was no time for questions as I heard the sound of Corrine struggling. "Have you lost your mind?" she shrilled. "What are you gaining by siding with the IBSI?"

I dashed to the entrance of the building and began scaling the stairs. My finger closed around the trigger of my gun. Corrine was powerful. She shouldn't need my help. But I feared the spell Loira had thrown at her while her back had been turned could have put her at a fatal disadvantage.

As their voices got louder and louder amidst crashing and smashing of glass, I had to bite my tongue to not yell out and attract attention toward myself, averting it from Corrine. If I was to stand any chance of helping Corrine, I needed an element of surprise on my side.

"I owe them a favor," came Loira's voice, surprisingly matter-of-fact. "It's really nothing personal, Corrine."

The two women shared a grunt as I imagined their spells clashing.

I reached their level, my blood pulsing in my ears as I stopped outside the door of the room they were in. I pressed my ear against it, trying to gauge the right moment to storm in. It was impossible. Although I could estimate their proximity from the door, it hardly helped me.

I just needed to barge in and do what I could.

Steadying my gun, I pulled down the door handle sharply and pushed myself inside. Corrine was clearly losing this battle. She was now pinned up against the wall by Loira, whose hands were closed around her throat. Hands that had begun to glow red, like hot iron.

Raising my gun, I aimed it at Loira's back. She'd better stay put, or my bullet could go right through to Corrine. I held my breath and pulled the trigger. Loira screamed and jerked backward. She fell to the ground, leaving Corrine to slide down the wall, clasping her throat.

I didn't know an awful lot about witches and their magic. For all I knew, Loira could quickly heal the bullet wound. As I locked eyes with Corrine, I was about to yell to her to finish the woman off while she could, but Corrine was already on the job. She staggered to her feet. I expected her to throw a curse down at Loira, but instead, she merely withdrew a knife from her belt. Leaping atop the woman, she slit her throat.

I hurried to her, staring down at the blood spilling from Loira's throat. Corrine's eyes glittered with anger as she rose, her hands soiled, her chest heaving.

She drew in a shuddering breath. "Thanks, Lawrence, I

owe you one," she said, wiping her sweaty forehead with her forearm. "This meddlesome witch can continue her meddling in Hell."

LAWRENCE

Corrine healed herself before she and I returned to the scene of the battle outside. I abandoned my idea of attempting to assist at ground level and instead let her soar me to the roof of a building that was closer to the fight.

It was just as hard to see through the smoke as it had been earlier, perhaps more so now, even despite the breeze carrying much of the smoke away.

I spotted dozens of mutants along with hunters scattered on the ground. My chest constricted as I spotted a fallen dragon, too. By the looks of it, he wasn't getting up again.

Who had been atop that dragon? How many more members of our army had we lost?

I looked toward the area in the sky where I had spotted the press reporters who'd hung back earlier in their choppers. There were still some there now, but less than before. Most appeared too afraid to hover here any longer. And rightly so. The scene was descending into a massacre.

I didn't think we could maintain this fight for much longer without risking too many lives. Especially when a massive explosion went off about half a mile away from us. I felt the heat of the blast against my skin, and it caused Corrine to retreat backward with me.

It caused the dragons to scatter. They could handle such heat, but their riders couldn't. I wasn't sure where Lethe was at this point—I couldn't make him out anywhere—but I hoped he was staying a good distance away.

Even with our magic wielders, we were outnumbered. There were too many of the IBSI's army for us to contend with, all of them darting through the sky in different directions at supernatural speed. More of their army had fallen than ours, judging by the sample of land beneath me now. But we weren't invincible.

More than anything I wondered what we truly had to gain by staying here any longer. We wouldn't eradicate the IBSI. We would only delay their reassertion of power over the city, and more lives would likely be lost in the process. Press were still watching, but I was sure that they would not be able to broadcast anything. It was looking more and more like an unnecessary endeavor.

I gazed at Corrine as the two of us grappled with what our next step should be. Now I saw doubt in the witch's eyes, doubt that had not been there before, when she'd made her statement that we couldn't leave. That we had to stay to assert our rebellion and not make reclaiming power so easy for the IBSI.

But now, it seemed that she was realizing what I had feared all along.

We had lost.

The two hours the authorities had given us to prove ourselves were up.

They had returned all power to the IBSI. TSL had been shut out. The golden window of opportunity we had so painstakingly opened up for ourselves had closed.

Our staying here longer seemed like mere stubbornness. And as much as I admired everyone's courage, there came a point when stubbornness turned into stupidity. I did not want to witness more people fall. Enough had died already due to the IBSI.

We had to recognize when to step back.

"I think we should retreat," I said, even as it killed me.

Corrine winced as though I'd slapped her. She pursed her lips tightly, her jaw twitching.

Maybe we would come upon another opportunity in the future to prove ourselves. But it wasn't now. Our timing from the start had been all off kilter. Ultimately, in spite of our intentions, we had caused more harm than good. I could hardly bear to think how many innocent lives had been affected, not just here in Chicago, but elsewhere where my father had ordered the boundaries to be pulled.

Another massive explosion sounded, closer this time, causing the dragons and all of us to retreat further. Then came another, and another—blasts spurting up from the ground like fiery fountains—until TSL had moved back so far, we were almost at the border of the river.

We had, in essence, already retreated.

Corrine gulped. "It looks like you're right, Lawrence."

We rose higher in the sky to avoid the scorching heat. Now I spotted Lethe. He had positioned himself atop a skyscraper on the other side of the river. I caught sight of his hunched-over figure, gazing in our direction. At least he'd kept himself a safe distance away.

We arrived among the rest of our group. The horde of mutants encroaching further, we found ourselves backing away together. The witches put up a protective spell around our group, so that they could not get too close while we hovered in the sky.

I gazed around at the ashen faces of my fellow fighters.

Our group was not as small as I'd feared it might be. Everyone I recognized had survived.

"We need to cut our losses now," I told them, raising my voice above the mutants' screams. The beasts and the hunters were attempting to break through the protection. They didn't just want to beat us back; they wanted to end us.

Everyone shared the same expression of deep reluctance. Of pain.

One of the dragons—Jeriad, I thought his name was— bellowed across the river to Lethe. *Crap.* The mutants had spotted the ice dragon again.

Corrine planted me on the back of Xavier's dragon before quickly vanishing herself toward Lethe, who had already taken Jeriad's warning and begun to flee. The witch reached him and put up a protective bubble around the two of them before returning and rejoining us beneath the main protective barrier.

"Are we all together?" Corrine croaked, doing a head count.

"Yes, we're all here," Rose's husband spoke up, a vampire whose name I had forgotten.

"What's the matter?" one of the hunters roared at us from outside. He had been so bold as to remove his protective mask, and now I realized that I recognized him. Oliver Hyatt was his name. He was one of my father's right-hand men. *So the IBSI's leaders are acting as foot soldiers after all.*

"Scared now?" Oliver continued to taunt. "I wish you'd realized you were out of your depth before you began all this." Gripping the reins of his mutant, he gestured to the destruction around us—the burning city, littered with bodies and broken buildings. "This is what your so-called holistic approach has led to."

The dragons rumbled at his words. Everyone tensed. My throat felt tight. I wished that I could shout back a retort, but I wasn't sure what could be said in this moment. His words were so twisted—completely ignoring the fact that the IBSI had been the ones to let down the boundaries in the first place—it was hard to know where to even start with such a man. Arguing or throwing back harsh words seemed utterly pointless. They'd only bounce off him.

"Go back to your little island and continue your pipe dreams," Oliver snarled. "Our friends at the press over there have recorded your failure enough to make the *world* want to hunt you down for your stupidity. I suggest you think carefully before leaving your base again."

As he pulled on the reins and moved to turn around— apparently realizing that there was no point in continuing to try to get at us with his men while we were protected—Rose called out, "Hey, *sir*. Where do you think you're going?"

Oliver, along with the rest of his army who had also started turning to leave, resumed his focus on us, his eyes locking on Rose. His face took on an expression of utter disdain.

"To clean up this mess you have created," Oliver shot back. "Unless you'd like to battle with us some more? We will oblige."

Rose glared daggers at him. I frowned as I stared at Grace's aunt. She had risen to her feet on the back of the dragon she shared with her husband to command Oliver's attention. I had no idea what was going through her head, why she was even bothering to talk to this piece of crap.

"I would like to ask you a couple of questions first," she countered. "Then we can talk about another battle."

I frowned even more deeply.

"What?" Oliver snapped, clearly impatient now.

"What's your name?"

"What?" Oliver replied, his face contorting with the same confusion as I felt.

Where is Rose going with this?

"It's a simple question," Rose retorted.

I half expected him to just turn around, continue on his way and ignore her. But apparently her odd behavior had piqued his interest in some small way.

"Oliver Hyatt," he replied.

"What would you do if you weren't working for the IBSI, Oliver?" she asked.

Oliver scoffed. "There is no other calling I would give my life to."

A wry smile curved the corners of Rose's mouth. Then she said in a soft voice, "I hope you're prepared for unemployment, Mr. Hyatt."

Her eyes rose above his head, and then I realized the cause of Rose's behavior.

Sweeping toward us like a dark storm in the distance was a throng of Hawks so large it blocked the moonlight.

As the hunters twisted around on their mutants to see what Rose was staring at, their jaws dropped.

It's not over yet, Father.

It's not over yet.

DEREK

Ibrahim, Horatio and I had an important journey ahead of us. We already had willing accomplices in the supernatural dimension—several species had pledged themselves to our cause, due to our freeing them from the hunters' grasp a short while ago. Now the time had finally come for us to call upon them.

We needed to gather an army large enough to convince the world that we had the manpower—or rather, the supernatural power—to take over from the IBSI. Not only to protect them from the Bloodless, but also to root out other mischievous supernaturals that the IBSI had still not been all that effective in controlling.

This was possibly the most epic task I had ever faced. But burning within me was deep confidence that we could pull this off. Our day had finally come. As night had for the IBSI.

Our first stop was The Woodlands. With Ibrahim keeping a spell of shadow over me, it didn't take us long to find a pack of werewolves who recognized me. We had spent a good deal of time here in helping them to drive out the IBSI, and I had met and spoken with many werewolves personally, from many tribes. We came across three members of the Turnfur tribe. We traveled by magic with them from pack to pack until we had gathered an army of hundreds of werewolves. Victoria was supposed to be hanging around somewhere here, with Mona and Brock. But we didn't come across her. Ironically, our last stop ended up being Blackhall Mountain, where they informed us that Victoria and Bastien had already left for The Shade. We must've narrowly missed them. The Blackhalls had appointed a new leader and were in the process of mourning due to recently losing some pack members. But they would be the last to forget all that they owed us. They joined us, too.

Once we were finished in The Woodlands, we moved next to The Trunchlands. The werewolves agreed to wait on the shore of the ogres' land while Ibrahim, Horatio and I ventured inside. It became apparent that the royal mountain kingdom that had previously been abandoned had been reoccupied. Thus we did not have to travel far or wide to find the king.

We entered the mountain and were met by some aggressive ogres who did not realize the deal we had made with their king, but once they had calmed down, they agreed to lead us to him. We followed them up through the mountain to the royal wing. Anselm Raskid emerged from his quarters, and on seeing us, his eyes instantly darkened. Apparently he had grown a tad complacent in the time that had passed since we had freed him and his people. He had probably been hoping that we would never call upon his help in the end. He'd been wrong.

"It is time for you to return a favor," I told him, looking the tall, rough-skinned man seriously in the eyes. "I am certain that you remember your promise."

He nodded, a slight grimace forming on his lips. "Yes, King Derek Novak. I have not forgotten."

"Then you must come with us now. We need you to gather as many ogres as you think are capable of being… reliable around humans."

I couldn't deny that I felt nervous about having ogres join our army. I trusted the werewolves well enough, but ogres? I feared what would happen if even one of them lost control and went on a human-eating rampage when we got to Earth.

That would be an absolute PR disaster for TSL. And the IBSI would try to milk the incident for all it was worth.

We had to prove the IBSI wrong in their belief that no supernaturals could be trusted, responsible beings. That they were incapable of helping solve Earth's problems. In spite of all that I'd been through and all that I'd seen in my long life—all the times I'd been betrayed and all the evil I had witnessed in people—I still preferred to give people, be they humans or supernaturals, the benefit of the doubt. Thus I placed my faith in Anselm to pick out an army who would do right by us, and control their nature, given all that we had done for them.

Of course, if he or any of his ogres messed up, there was always the threat that TSL would come after them, just as we had come after the hunters. They knew that we had a fierce army of dragons… That alone should be enough to make them control their nature and deter any of them from taking a misstep.

Once the king had summoned his army, we headed to the beach to join the werewolves. It was interesting watching the werewolves and ogres interact, or rather not interact. Apart from Bella and Brett on our island, I didn't think I'd ever seen how werewolves responded to the presence of ogres and vice versa. The two species stared at each other from across a stretch of sand, both of them apparently distrusting—

particularly the ogres, oddly.

I cast my eyes over the ogres and set my gaze on the king, who was looking no more enthusiastic than his kinsmen about the prospect of joining forces with the werewolves.

"I suggest that you warm to each other," I said pointedly. "Because soon you will be cooperating with many other species—including dragons."

The king nodded, his lips forming a hard line.

Next, we headed to The Sanctuary. Although we had played no part in saving the witches recently, they owed us a lifetime of debt already. First, for ending the black witches practically single-handedly a couple of decades ago, and secondly, for my daughter having rescued one of the royal sisters. We'd had decent, amenable dealings with them ever since.

I experienced intense déjà vu as we arrived on the shore of the witches' country. We had come to seek out Loira Sulvece only days ago to assist us in discovering the Hawk-vampire boys.

Ibrahim took the initiative to call out through the boundary for somebody to attend to us. A youngish blond warlock with shoulder-length hair emerged.

Ibrahim seemed to recognize him. "Coen," he addressed the man. "We need to speak with the Ageless."

"What is it about?" he asked. His eyes bulged as he took

in the beach jam-packed with supernaturals.

"We need to borrow some of you," Ibrahim replied before adding, "We need to speak to her urgently."

"Hm, all right," Coen said. His eyes traveled once again, up and down the beach. "It seems that it will be easier if I bring her to you. I will head to her palace at once."

"So," Ibrahim said, turning to me as Coen vanished. "How many witches do you think we should bring?"

I ran a hand through my hair, eyeing our army thus far. Witches were probably the most valuable kind of supernatural we could gather. "As many as possible."

"Right," Ibrahim muttered, nodding.

We waited for about fifteen minutes before the oldest Adrius sister arrived on the beach. The current Ageless.

She bowed her head to me courteously as she approached in a long silver gown, her fair hair trailing down her shoulders.

"Good day, King Derek," she said, bowing her head slightly. "And Ibrahim." Her eyes passed over the warlock. Although she looked at Horatio, too, and I was quite sure that she knew his name, she chose not to greet him. The witches of The Sanctuary still had some way to go to catch up with the witches of The Shade in regards to their relations with and prejudices against jinn.

Just like the ogres and werewolves, this was a prejudice

they were going to need to snap out of fast.

"We require witches to accompany us to Earth," I began. "As many as you can spare. As you can see"—I gestured to the supernaturals packing the sand—"we are building a multifaceted army. I'm sure that you are aware of the IBSI and their general dealings on Earth—and in the supernatural dimension."

"More so in the supernatural dimension," the Ageless replied, wetting her lower lip. "My people have not had many dealings with Earth recently, as you know."

"Well, you are about to have a whole lot more." I explained to the witch all that we planned to accomplish as quickly as I could, while giving as much detail as was required for her to bite.

Once I finished, she nodded slowly. "I understand your requirements... While I cannot guarantee you any specific number of my people, I will call an urgent meeting now, and I will gather as many volunteers as I can."

White witches were not known to be the most selfless of beings. As she vanished, I had to hope that she could provide a substantial number. We had a staggering amount of work to do. And although I held out hope that, on seeing TSL's growing army, some of the IBSI members would jump ship. Jennifer Thornton had suspected many in the IBSI weren't happy in their roles within the organization and would welcome the chance to leave. Unfortunately, we could not pin our hopes on that. That would be a bonus.

It really would be a boon though if many IBSI members did join us. They would be extremely valuable in the early days, because they already had internal structures in place. We could learn from their systems while building upon and improving them.

When the Ageless finally returned, an uncomfortable amount of time had passed. To say that we did not have forever was an understatement. I had not been able to give Xavier or my son a specific time frame for when we would return, for that was impossible. There were so many variables on this supernatural side of the universe. All I could tell them was that we would do our utmost to return with an army as soon as physically possible.

I was pleasantly surprised by the number of witches and warlocks who arrived—over a couple of hundred. These would compliment our current group of magic wielders nicely.

It had occurred to me that more jinn would also be extremely useful, but unfortunately, those were not creatures we had any leverage with, and certainly not ones that we wanted to meddle with.

The beach was so packed now that the ogres had retreated into the sea in order to make room for everybody to stand.

Witches, ogres, and werewolves, oh my.

But we were not done yet.

We had two more ports of call—the next being The Hearthlands. That visit would not be challenging at all, given our friendly relations with King Theon. We had become like family over the years, even though we lived worlds apart. Theon had come to visit with his wife Penelope and brother Altair on occasion, staying in the dragons' quarters in the Black Heights. And their invitation was always open to us; indeed, my son's wedding had taken place there. Although The Shade and The Hearthlands were two nations, we were as good as one.

The ogres were understandably jittery about our next stop, but I assured them that it would be a good... exercise in trust for them. I promised them that none of the dragons would harm them, so long as they harmed no humans when we returned to Earth—and I trusted the dragons enough to uphold that assurance.

Thus, the witches transported us all to the verdant land of The Hearthlands. We landed outside the royal castle. Before entering, I took a moment to gaze about the town, nestled among rolling green hills and valleys. It was in moments like this that I wished I could be human again, enjoy the feeling of the sun on my skin. But henceforward, I would remain a vampire. I couldn't keep switching; I'd done so too many

A DAY OF GLORY

times before. The body built up resistance to the cure—the last time I had tried, I'd almost died. Since then I had promised Sofia that I would remain as I was. Forever a vampire, like her.

I breathed in deep, relishing the fragrant air for a few seconds while clearing my head of the dizziness that sometimes accompanied magical travel.

Then, followed by Ibrahim and Horatio, I approached the front door and knocked. A guard opened the heavy oaken doors and, instantly recognizing us, his face lit up.

"Come in! Come in!"

"Thank you," I told him, smiling in appreciation. "But first of all, please cast your eyes upon my fellow travelers." I gestured behind me. The guard's lips parted as he took in the supernaturals crowding the town. Particularly the ogres.

"You see, we have arrived with companions. I have come to speak to your king, but I need you to ensure us that no attempts are made by your dragons to snap at our ogre friends while we are inside the castle."

I could practically see the hunger in the guard's eyes as he gazed at the ogres, even in his humanoid form. He returned to his senses and looked back to me. "Of course, Your Highness. It shall be done."

The guard looked over his shoulder and barked behind him, beckoning over more guards. He explained to them that the ogres were with us, and they agreed to stand outside and make sure that any other passing dragons were aware that the ogres were not to be touched.

Then the first guard who had greeted us led Horatio, Ibrahim and me into the magnificent castle. He seated us in a richly furnished waiting room. He offered us refreshments, which we politely refused. We had no time to indulge in the luxuries of the dragon kingdom.

We were waiting for only five minutes by my calculation before Theon burst into the room. His thick wavy hair grazing his shoulders, his chiseled face lit up in a brilliant smile that illuminated his golden eyes.

"Derek!" he boomed.

He crossed the room to greet me with a hearty hug and a slap on the back that practically knocked the wind out of me.

I returned the embrace before gripping his shoulders and creating a few inches of distance between us.

"Theon. The time has come where we need your help more than ever before."

I was only a couple of minutes into explaining why we needed his help when he agreed unconditionally to provide us with as many dragons as we needed for our mission.

"Good man," I said, squeezing his shoulders. "I suggest that every dragon who is willing to help us head to The Shade immediately." I had to be mindful that the dragons were not ones to travel by magic. That meant that they would need more time. They could be traveling to The Shade while we finished up in our journey.

Theon escorted us to the castle exit before bidding us farewell—for now. Then he closed the door, hurrying off to begin giving orders.

Now it was time for us to head to our fifth and final destination.

Aviary.

Of course, there were many other supernaturals who could have come in use to us, but these five were the only ones we had leverage with for now. I hoped that in the future this would change, and we could turn still more supernaturals into forces for good. Into guardians, rather than threats.

As we returned to the area outside the castle where the witches, werewolves and ogres were waiting, I thanked the dragon guards and said that they would likely be wanted in the castle now.

My gaze swept over the ogres. They let out silent sighs of relief as the dragons placed distance between them and disappeared into the castle. They looked infinitely grateful to move on.

Everybody gathered close together and the witches transported us away from The Hearthlands.

When our feet hit solid ground again, we were surrounded by the sweltering heat of Aviary. We had arrived in the midst of a jungle.

I turned to Ibrahim. "Now, I suggest that you wait here with the witches, werewolves and ogres, while Horatio and I go to gather the Hawks."

The last time we had been here together in Aviary, we had only brought back fifty Hawks. There were many more we could find use for now.

Horatio rose with me in the sky. We gazed over the ocean of treetops, trying to get our bearings. Horatio, thankfully, had a better sense of direction than I did. It took us less time than I had feared it might to locate the new city of Aviary, if the makeshift colonization could be called such.

As we passed the rickety homes, we called out to the Hawks. Many of them recognized me from the speech I had made only a short while ago. I requested all of them to head to the same circular platform as before, and once several hundred had gathered around, I began to address them. I explained to them that The Shade and their fellow Hawks who still remained with us needed their help urgently, and all who came with us would have The Shade's, and indeed, Earth's, eternal gratitude. Even as I spoke, I couldn't get over how strange it felt to be requesting Hawks to become guardians of the Earth, when only several decades ago they had been practically as manipulative to humans as the Elders.

But they agreed. They agreed, I supposed, because they heard the passion in my voice, the sincerity and earnestness with which I called them to arms. Even though they were shadows of their former selves in terms of confidence and aggression, I trusted that, when the time came and we were all together, they would rediscover the strength that had once made them feared warriors.

Finally, the IBSI would receive the comeuppance that was long overdue.

As soon as a large group of the Hawks had assembled, Horatio and I returned with them to where we had left Ibrahim and the rest of our army. After introducing them briefly—barely having time to watch everybody's reaction to our new members, particularly the witches, who had a history of discord with Aviary—I announced that it was time for us to return to The Shade. There, we would reunite with the rest of the Hawks, along with the dragons who should have arrived by now. And finally, I would touch base to see what had been happening with my son and the rest of the League. They were supposed to be infiltrating the media and should have done a thorough job by now. They'd had plenty of time.

When we all returned to the island, naturally, we had to bypass our usual rules of having witches check that nobody was an imposter—I knew that they weren't, and it would be far too time-consuming now. Ibrahim allowed us inside, and our army lined up on the beach by the Port, where the dragons were thankfully already waiting—including Theon and his brother Altair. I noticed only three ice dragons among them, which was probably wise, given the mutants we might be forced to face.

I told everyone to wait on the beach for my next instruction, and had Horatio stay to keep an eye on everyone, while Ibrahim went to transport weapons and armor from the Armory.

I first hurried to Eli and Shayla's apartment, which he had left open for me. He had access to more television channels than anyone on the island, but as I began to flick through them, all of the major ones were blank. I had to switch into channels located outside of the United States to discover what had been going on, and as I watched the reporters relaying the news, I swore beneath my breath.

The IBSI had brought down the borders of not only Chicago, but New York and Los Angeles. *Dammit!* At the back of my mind, I had been fearing that Atticus would do something rash like this. My heart pounded. We had to get a move on, and my gut instinct was telling me that our first port of call had to be Chicago. That was where Ben and the others were first due to head.

I hurried out of Eli's apartment and fetched the rest of the Hawks, who were staying in temporary accommodations. I directed them to wait by the Port with the others before I dashed to the Black Heights to see if any of our resident dragons were here. None were.

I hurtled back to the Port, and, standing atop the jetty which gave me a vantage point over our entire army gathered on the sand, I bellowed, "We must leave as soon as possible!"

Ibrahim had already returned with what looked like our entire stock of weapons and begun distributing them to the Hawks along with armor. Ibrahim demonstrated how to use the guns, something that took patience I didn't have in this moment. The ogres had brought their own weapons with them, and as for the werewolves, they couldn't hold weapons anyway in their wolf forms.

Once Ibrahim was done with the demonstration, he and Horatio arrived at my side.

"We need to head to Chicago," I told them. "We can meet near the same news station Ben and the others were due to head to first. Horatio, you should accompany the dragons. They will travel fast, but not fast enough for the rest of us. Guide the dragons there. Ibrahim and I, along with everybody else, will travel by magic. Is that all right?"

Horatio and Ibrahim nodded.

I barked out orders to everybody. The dragons parted

from the crowd and approached Horatio, while Ibrahim and I mingled with the rest of the army.

A few seconds later, The Shade disappeared.

* * *

Arriving at our destination, it was clear that things had gone even worse than I thought they had. Much worse. The building had been blown up, ash and debris coating the street that lined it.

What happened here?

I needed to scope out the city to figure out what was going on. I took to the sky on the back of one of the Hawks, rising above the buildings, where I witnessed even more destruction. In the distance, the residential area of the city was ablaze—buildings smashed and charred, bodies strewn everywhere. And then, still further, near the river, I spotted a massive horde of hunters riding atop mutants. In front of them were my people. It was clear that the League was under the protection of a spell, for the mutants could not approach closer than a dozen feet.

I flew with the Hawk back to where I had left the others and climbed off the Hawk.

"Right," I said, my heart hammering. "We can't wait for the dragons. We've got to go in now and eradicate the IBSI."

I explained that I wanted to do this in stages. In waves. First I would arrive with the Hawks. We would launch the attack on the mutants in the sky, draw their attention toward us. And following us immediately would be the witches. Only once we had managed to successfully take the hunters out of the sky could we have our ground army of ogres and werewolves surge forward and sweep the streets for survivors, assisting any innocent humans, while felling any IBSI members—assuming they did not surrender.

But where was the press now? It was vital that the scene was recorded so that the public could see our strength. I noticed some helicopters in the distance, but I wasn't sure what they were.

"Ibrahim." I addressed the warlock. "I would like you to keep an eye on the stages of the battle. Let everybody know when to enter in turn. And once everybody here has left for the battlefield, stay here and wait for the dragons. They shouldn't take too long. When they arrive you can send them to us immediately, and you can join us too. Is that all right?"

"Yes, Derek," Ibrahim replied.

I drew in a breath before turning to the Hawks. I climbed onto the back of a Hawk who carried two guns. I took one from him and held it in one hand. As we rose up, I fished in my pocket for my phone and switched it to camera mode. In case there was nobody else recording, I could capture everything from a close-up perspective. A very close-up perspective.

We flew over the buildings and hurtled toward the river. My Hawk flew at the front of the flock, and there were so many of us, we stretched out in the sky like an ominous cloud. I pointed toward the direction of the mutants. We sped up, closing the gap, even as everyone prepared their guns.

We managed to make good ground before the IBSI noticed us. I caught sight of my daughter, her eyes trained on me, a few moments before everybody else looked in our direction.

"Brace yourselves," I roared, as the hunters began firing. It was difficult to shoot properly with one hand, but I was going to have to manage it for as long as possible.

If we could show that we were strong enough to defeat the IBSI in their own territory, then we were strong enough to defeat everything that the IBSI was capable of defeating.

I was grateful to Ibrahim for taking the time to train the Hawks. As swift and vicious as they were capable of being— and I had first-hand experience of their strength while saving Sofia from the clutches of Arron, many, many years ago— they were not scaled like dragons and were still vulnerable to bullets.

We fired our guns toward the IBSI. I was focused on the

man who appeared to be leading them all. I couldn't be sure who it was, for he wore a mask, but I wondered if perhaps it might be Atticus.

As the hunters' firing intensified, the mutants' screeches piercing the night, the witches surged behind us. They quickly created a massive invisible shield around us that caused all the bullets shooting our way to bounce off and go hurtling in the opposite direction—some even making it back to the IBSI.

Let's see how much you feel like firing now.

The hunters' confidence broke. They stopped rushing toward us so quickly. Gripping the reins of their mutants, they pulled them back, retracing their flight in the sky. The League behind them took advantage of the distraction we had caused and began to close in on them from their side, too. Realizing that we were trapping them in a deadly sandwich, the hunters began to drop down to the city for shelter.

Some shelter they'll find down there.

Ibrahim was supposed to be monitoring the scene, and seeing them descend should trigger him to send in our ground warriors... though, on second thought, it was still too early for that. We hadn't managed to injure enough mutants yet. Not nearly enough. Although they were closer to ground level, the hunters were still using the beasts to shoot about, either by running or by flying low to the ground. I feared that it was still too dangerous for the ogres and werewolves to come in. They were no match for the mutants' fire.

Forced to pause my filming, I dialed Ibrahim's number. He picked up after a single ring.

"Wait before you send in the rest," I told him. "We need to weaken the mutants first and get more IBSI members on the ground before we're ready for them. Though as soon as the dragons arrive, you can send them in."

Ibrahim agreed to keep everybody on standby. I hung up.

"Where are you going?" I bellowed down to a group of hunters scattering with their mutants around the buildings. "Come back and defend your right to rule!"

It was a smart move on their part to move to the ground, at least as smart a move as they could make given the circumstances we'd put them in.

It was easier for them to spread themselves out here. They could hide behind buildings and pop out at unexpected moments. It was hard for the League's army to travel together in one solid, shielded block because of this. We were forced to split up in order to go chasing after the hunters. The landscape divided us, making us weaker. But not weak enough.

Yells and bullets ricocheted off the buildings, the

atmosphere alight with tension.

The hunters might have made this a more drawn-out process for us, but they weren't going to escape now. Going into this, a part of me had been hoping that they would flee the scene of the battle when witnessing the scale of our people, flee back to their base, which would be basically admitting surrender to us. But these hunters were tougher, more stubborn than that. It looked like they planned to stay and fight to the very end.

I caught sight of Sofia riding atop Neros. Relief shone in her eyes as they locked with mine.

I addressed the Hawk. "Can you transfer me to that dragon, please?"

Once the Hawk drew close enough, I leapt onto his back, sliding myself behind my wife. I slipped an arm around her waist, pressing my lips against the back of her cool neck.

"I thought you'd failed," she said breathlessly.

I squeezed her, *tsk*ing. "And I thought you knew me better than that, Mrs. Novak. Failure is not a word in my dictionary."

Lawrence

Everyone let out audible sighs of relief when Derek's army came into view. He'd made it. Late. But he'd made it nonetheless. Now we were going to have to do the best that we could to salvage the situation.

As the fighting started up again and we launched at the hunters with renewed strength—myself sharing a dragon with Kiev—I glanced over at the press helicopters. They inched a tad closer as our new flurry of activity started. I hoped that they would draw closer still.

Although the dragon was leading us to rejoin the battle, I had something more important to do first. I requested the dragon to drop me off on the roof of a building about a mile away—away from the epicenter of the danger. I broke open the door to a stairwell leading down into the building and took a seat on one of the steps so that I could make a phone call without distraction.

I dialed the old government official's number. Fowler was his name.

I feared that he might not even pick up. But he did, after five rings.

"It's Lawrence," I said immediately. "Don't hang up. There's been a development. Our backup has arrived and we're driving the IBSI out of their own territory as we speak. We will win and take control of the Chicago situation. We will then do the same with New York. Get back over here, and you can witness the same for yourself. Or, better still, allow the reporters to continue doing their damn job. You never should've shut them down to begin with."

There was a pause on the other end of the line. I could hear the man's uneven breathing. "I-I'll have a reporter stream footage to us," he said, "so we can verify the situation for ourselves."

"Be our guest," I told him.

With that, I hung up. A feeling of satisfaction swelled within me as I gazed down at the phone.

I knew that Fowler would not waste time in verifying the

facts himself. They were just as desperate as we were to see the backs of the IBSI. They wanted us to take over; they simply needed us to prove that we were capable of it.

And finally, we were.

Once he'd verified the situation, we should be back on track with our original plan.

I slipped the phone back into my pocket and returned to the roof. I gazed up at the sky, looking for a dragon, a witch, or even a Hawk, who could swoop down to pick me up and allow me to rejoin the battle.

With a deafening shriek, something did swoop down— sooner than I even saw it coming.

The next thing I knew, I was trapped within the talons of a mutant, and hurtling over a several-hundred-feet freefall.

BEN

Once Atticus's men came for him, we knew that the clock was ticking in regards to how much longer we could keep him hostage. Either we had to get rid of the distraction, or leave, allowing Atticus to go free.

I was unwilling to do the latter. As they burst through the door of Atticus's office, Kailyn and I launched at the men. Taking them by surprise, we slammed books into their heads, knocking them out. This bought us some more time. We dragged them into the hallway and left them there unconscious.

Then we returned to Atticus, who was still looking fairly

calm. He'd scored a victory in getting all of the major news channels shut down. And even though he was trapped in here with us, unable to make contact with anyone outside, he knew what was happening now. Just like we did. The IBSI would be in the process of regaining control. But we weren't ready to leave yet. Not now that we had him. I was still holding out hope that my father would arrive, albeit late. And as the news channels suddenly flickered on again, depicting an epic battle taking place in Chicago's residential quarters, my hope was realized.

"Thank heavens!" Kailyn exclaimed, moving closer to the screen and gaping.

My father had arrived with an army of Hawks and witches. On witnessing the sheer number of supernaturals he'd brought with him, I felt a resurgence of confidence.

We can do this. I know we can!

My eyes shot to Atticus, still bound to his chair. "Well," I taunted, "what do you make of this?"

His face was stony, and as much as I could tell that he was trying to hide his dismay, emotions trickled through.

He did not respond.

I snatched up the landline on his desk.

"It's over," I told him. "Can't you see? Tell your men to withdraw now and you will spare many of your employees' lives." *Not that you care.*

Atticus's mouth remained pressed in a hard line. Witnessing the IBSI members continuing to put up a fight was a disappointment to me. In the face of such an army as my father had summoned, I was hoping that some would've surrendered. But from the looks of it, none had. Perhaps we needed to fight them longer before they dared to jump ship. Assert our superiority beyond a shadow of a doubt. I imagined the brainwashing they would've received from the organization, and the fear in their hearts if they ever broke away from it. Considering the IBSI's history of tracking people down and assassinating them, I could hardly blame them.

I glared at Atticus. "Well, in that case, perhaps we will take you outside to give you a better view."

LAWRENCE

The mutant flew with me over the streets, flying at such an angle that I struggled to even twist around within its grasp. But when I managed it, I found myself gazing up at a hunter. Oliver Hyatt, no less. He wasn't wearing his mask, and as I glanced up at him, he glared down at me.

"You started all this, Lawrence," he said, his voice menacing.

Reaching another roof, the mutant dropped me. I fell to the ground, softening my fall with my forearms, before shooting to my feet. When I had been swept up by the mutant, the shock of it had caused me to drop my gun. I still had my blades tucked into my belt, but as Oliver stepped off the mutant and advanced toward me, he was holding a gun.

"What do you think you will gain by shooting me?" I asked him. "Do you think my father will be pleased?"

The answer to that was probably yes, but I was curious to hear it from his own lips.

"Whether or not your father would be pleased," the man replied, "doesn't matter. Because he will never know." His lips curled. "The dead don't talk, Lawrence."

Oliver pulled the trigger, a bullet shooting from the barrel. With my supernatural speed, I managed to duck in time before it could hit me. I jerked backward, across the roof, and threw myself behind a cluster of thick pipes.

I reached for the knives in my belt and pulled them out. Then, both swiftly and cautiously, I raised my head slightly to glimpse the approaching hunter. He fired again. I ducked, the bullet bouncing off a metal pipe, only inches away from my ear.

"You're wasting your time," I called out.

Crouching low, I moved to my right along the pipes, to the edge of the roof. The reason for my uttering that particular statement was to mark my location in his mind— before hurrying away from it. My trick worked. As I poked my head up again, he was still watching the area where I had spoken, giving me the chance to raise one of my knives and hurl it in Oliver's direction.

But to my alarm, he dodged it in time.

There was no way that he could've done that had he been a normal human. The knife would've hit him square in the chest.

Instead he moved as swiftly as I was capable of moving. He must have taken the enhancement drug too. He was on my level.

Dammit.

I tightened my grip around the handle of my remaining blade. My eyes raked the sky. A dragon or a Hawk hanging around here would really come in useful right now. But I could not depend on being saved.

"Why don't you throw the other knife, Lawrence?" Oliver's voice spoke behind me. "I'm ready for it."

He shot another bullet in my direction. It wasn't safe to take shelter behind this cluster of pipes any longer. I loped across the roof, dodging as he fired more bullets my way. I threw myself behind the wall of a rectangular storage chamber. Perhaps for gas or electricity. I knew that this was going to be a short-lived game of hide and seek. I had to get off this roof. I heard his footsteps circling the walls. I inched around, leading him along, until I found myself on the side of the mutant.

That mutant. As I stared at it now, I realized that I

recognized it—*him*. It was Jez. He was a popular choice for IBSI leaders to take out on a ride because of his obedience and easy-going nature compared to the other younger beasts.

The fact that he didn't immediately launch at me again when he saw me told me that he recognized me too. He had scooped me up before because it had been an order from his rider, but now that he had no rider... He was showing no signs of wanting to attack me.

Attempting to buy myself some more time and come up with a plan, I circled the walls again, to avoid Oliver.

When I roamed around the walls for a third time and the mutant came into view, still waiting in the same spot, I was about to simply launch myself at him, deeming that the best way out of the situation. But I stalled as Oliver shouted out in frustration, "Oh, come on, Lawrence. Stop running away. I didn't know you were such a coward."

Says the man holding a gun.

"I'll drop my gun if you like. Why don't you fight me, man to man?"

I swallowed. I didn't like the idea of running away, either. I would much rather face him and finish him off if that was what it took to get him off my tail.

"Throw your gun away then," I told him. "Throw it toward the mutant, where I can see it."

I was surprised when Oliver did exactly that. That could

have just been a trick by me—have him throw it there before I scooped it up. But apparently he believed that I had enough integrity to not do that. And I did. I respected him for putting the gun down. I didn't put my own blade down in turn, however. I wasn't that stupid. He could still be equipped with some hidden weapon because I hadn't searched him yet.

I peered around the corner cautiously to check that he did not have a second gun on his person. He didn't.

He was standing in the middle of the roof. He had nothing in his hands. He rolled up his sleeves as he glared at me. Then he raised a brow. "Not going to put down your own weapon?"

"Turn around," I told him.

He did so, and since I couldn't see any telltale signs of a weapon on him, I placed my weapon down. The mutant let out a squawk as the two of us began to circle. Our eyes locked.

He leapt forward first, rushing at me with his fists bared. He swung a punch at me, but I blocked, just as swiftly. Then I went in for the takedown. Throwing myself at his knees, I floored him before crawling on top of him. We each moved as fast as the other as he struggled to break free while I fought to maintain my control over him. I managed to knee him in the groin, weakening him, while catching his neck in a firm hold. In spite of all the evil he was responsible for perpetrating, I couldn't say that I truly wanted to kill him. I was tired of bloodshed. I had witnessed enough not just for one day, but for one lifetime.

But as Oliver managed to break free of my hold enough to shoot a hand up to my throat, it was clear that he saw this as a fight to the death, not just fight till surrender. And so it appeared that I had no choice but to play his game.

I moved upward abruptly, managing to jerk away from his grip. He shot to his feet after me. I landed a kick against his chest, forcing him backward toward the edge of the building. I surged forward, taking advantage of his unsteadiness, and managed to throw another kick, forcing him a few feet further backward still, until he managed to ground himself. He lunged and landed a punch on my left cheek, so hard that I felt my skin split. At least it hadn't landed on my nose. A punch that powerful to my nose would've debilitated me for several seconds.

He hurled himself at me, aiming for my throat again. As I fought him off, I deliberately moved him closer toward the roof's perimeter.

I wanted to make this quick now. I had other matters to attend to. I wanted to see what was going on with the others, and I also wondered where my father was now: what Ben had done, or was still doing, to him.

Oliver sensed what my game plan was. He attempted to move forward, keep us away from the edge, but I kept inching us nearer. This was, of course, also risky for me. If he got the advantage over me, I could be the one plunging down the side of the building, falling God knew how many feet and splattering on the pavement.

It was a calculated risk.

I aimed for his groin again with my knee, knowing that second shot would weaken him considerably. But he managed to block it, noticing my aim too soon.

He caught me again in the cheek, the same spot he caught last time, tearing my skin further. I felt the blood flowing down my face and trailing to my neck. I had to be careful not to be caught in the eye—it would swell up almost instantly from the force of the impact.

I returned the punch, catching him in the jaw and sending him reeling backward. He tripped over a pipe and fell. Here, I saw my golden opportunity. I pounced on him, grabbing him by the collar while he was still recovering from my punch, and dragged him toward the edge of the building. I kneed him again, this time managing to hit his groin. He groaned as I fought to wrestle him over the edge.

He grabbed hold of my arms, as I'd been expecting him to. If he was going down, he wanted me to go with him.

Perhaps he was not aware that I had experience with the

particular mutant that he had brought along with him. Or more likely, he was simply too distracted to think of it. Whatever the case, I let out a sharp whistle through my teeth that Jez was used to obeying from me.

Now that he had no other rider, he was a free agent. He came flying over to us. On realizing what I was doing, Oliver struggled harder, continuing his attempts to force me back, return the fight to the center of the roof. But I fought with all I had to keep him where he was now that I'd gotten him so close to the edge. I needed a little help from Jez to finish off the job.

As the mutant approached, I drove a hand into the tough feathers around his neck and held onto him for support as I thrust a kick against the man's gut. This proved to be effective in breaking his hold on me. He tipped backward, his upper half reeling over the edge. His feet still on the ground, I dropped down and grabbed his ankles. I lifted them upward abruptly to tip him over completely.

But when he was seconds from falling, his right arm shot down and grabbed the back of my shirt. As he began to fall, I didn't have enough warning to tear the shirt off myself. I found myself being tugged with him, toppling over the edge.

And then the two of us were falling.

The dull gray concrete beneath us was the sight of death. My life flashed before me. Oliver's scream pierced my ears as he plunged beside me. Then came another scream that was neither Oliver's nor my own.

It was a shriek that came from above. As I was barely seven feet from hitting the ground, strong talons closed around my shoulders. With a lurch that felt like it dislocated both of my shoulders, I was brought to an abrupt stop, about five feet over the pavement.

Oliver was not so lucky.

He hit the ground with a sickening splat and disintegrated like a ripe tomato. Tearing my eyes away from his mangled body, I gazed up at my savior. Jez could've saved either of us; we were both his masters. Yet he'd chosen to save me.

I supposed somewhere along the line, I must've treated him better. Something I was *dearly* thankful for.

He lowered me to the ground gently, where I collapsed for a few moments, my legs shaking from the shock. I had definitely injured my shoulders. I could hardly move them without pain shooting down my arms. But that shouldn't be anything one of the witches couldn't fix in a jiffy.

I glanced at Jez as he moved closer to me, and inhaled slowly. "Okay, friend. Let's get back to business."

DEREK

We finally managed to debilitate enough of the mutants to allow the ogres and werewolves to make an entrance. They came sweeping through the city like a tsunami, the werewolves growling, the ogres bellowing, as they destroyed any remaining IBSI members who had not yet surrendered... And indeed, in the process of taking down the mutants, a number of the IBSI members had finally realized that it was in their best interest to jump ship.

We gathered every surrendered man and woman together on two roofs. Ibrahim and Horatio kept an eye on them to be sure they meant what they said, and weren't about to try anything funny.

Throughout the fight, more and more helicopters had arrived and dared to move closer to watch. Lights flashed from the aircrafts; they were reporters, rendering my little camera defunct. I'd caught enough footage by now anyway, and when I had joined Sofia on her dragon, she had taken over filming for a while.

We had more than enough to demonstrate the IBSI's ass-kicking.

Now that we had mostly finished the battle in the sky, it was important for us to monitor what was going on at ground level with the ogres and the werewolves. I still felt uneasy about the ogres in particular. I caught sight of Anselm, who, to my surprise, was at the front of the ogre army, leading them forward as they coursed through street after street. I'd deliberately had the werewolves come in first. I trusted them more around humans. They searched within what was left of the buildings, and managed to find a few stray humans who had managed to survive in spite of the blaze, though, sadly, far more dead bodies were found than live ones.

All along, I had been prepared for more IBSI recruits to come swooping down on us. After all, they had members spread all over the United States. It would not have taken

BELLA FORREST

them all that long to assemble another army to come in to counteract us. But I believed, on witnessing the destruction that we had caused, they had decided against it. They had witnessed our army—so massive and multifaceted that even with all their mutants they simply couldn't compete. We had so many dragons now who could easily tackle the mutants, not to mention all the witches and Hawks, along with our ground army. It seemed that, finally, the day had come when their egos had been beaten down to size. The IBSI had realized that they were no match for TSL.

All this was just another reason why it was so important for us to have our activities broadcast. We needed not only the world to witness our strength and organization, but also the other IBSI's bases. Once we had finished dealing with Chicago, we would need to move on to the other affected cities, New York and Los Angeles, and then beyond. Hopefully, after this, the IBSI would not put up a fight there. But more than anything, I hoped that after this, their government support would be withdrawn. Something I was sure the authorities would've done long ago, if only they'd had a viable alternative.

I believed today was that day. A day of glory. A milestone in history. Not just for us, but for the world. Although we had much, much more work ahead of us—we had not even scratched the surface—this one battle would have an ongoing effect, and as dramatic as it sounded, it would alter the world's future.

I was drawn from my thoughts by an ogre roaring up to me, "Can I eat this human?"

My eyes shot toward him. An obese ogre if ever I saw one, his meaty hands were clamped around the skull of a stray IBSI member, who was struggling to break free from his grip.

I frowned in disdain at the ogre. At least he knew to ask permission from me. That much, I supposed, was commendable.

"No!" I barked down gruffly. "IBSI member or not, you're not allowed to eat anybody."

We had given permission to the ogres to kill our enemies, but not to eat them. They needed to get in the habit of abstaining from human flesh while they were on Earth, because I feared eating one man could lead to eating another, and then another, until they spiraled out of control and began eating innocents too.

"Please! I surrender!" the IBSI member gasped as he flailed.

I leapt from the dragon and landed next to the ogre and his struggling victim. My heart softened a little as I noted how young the IBSI man was. He didn't look much older than twenty. I was sure that he had loved ones somewhere waiting for him to come home.

"Let him go," I ordered the ogre.

The ogre huffed but relinquished his grip on him, sending him crumpling to the ground unceremoniously. I towered over the man, my arms crossed over my chest.

"Give me a reason to spare your life," I said, my menacing tone masking any softness I might've been feeling inside.

"I renounce the IBSI, and everything it stands for! I will do whatever you ask of me. Please. Just don't kill me."

"Do you understand why it was wrong to align yourself with the IBSI to begin with?" I prodded.

He nodded.

"Explain to me why."

"Because they never used the power they had for good. They exploited it. They piled resources into methods that were against the interest of the general population."

"Hm. Well said... All right. You will be spared."

He let out a deep gasp of relief, while the ogre looked rather disappointed that he couldn't at least take a swipe at the man's skull with his club.

"Move along," I told the ogre. "There's still work to be done."

I allowed the IBSI member to climb onto Neros's back with Sofia and me. We soared him toward a rooftop where some of his colleagues were waiting.

"Mom! Dad!"

Sofia and I twisted around toward the voice of our son behind us. He was soaring toward our rooftop with Kailyn and… Atticus. He was sandwiched in the middle of the two fae as they carried him.

His hands strapped behind his back by makeshift cuffs, Atticus's lined face was stoic. He refused to look me in the eye. He seemed to have already sensed that the game was up. I wondered how long he, Kailyn and Ben had been watching the scene.

I leapt off Neros and came face to face with the man who had caused the world so much grief and suffering. I stroked my jaw. *Interesting. Very interesting.*

"What do you think we should do with him?" Ben asked, an unmistakable spark of triumph in his eyes. He had a particular bone to pick with Atticus, given everything Atticus had put poor Grace through.

As I mulled over the matter, I could think of many things that I would like to do with this man. *Oh, decisions, decisions.* Lock him in a cage with a Bloodless? Throw him to our ogres and inform them that he was the one and only exception to my no-human-eating rule? Or maybe even make a special little trip to the ghouls' portal on the coast of Maine? If anybody deserved "time out" in The Underworld, it was Atticus.

I was about to ask Ben for his opinion when a loud thump

sounded to our left. I was shocked to see a mutant descend in our midst and immediately sprang into defense mode... until I realized that atop the mutant was Lawrence.

He looked like he'd been through the mill. His face was bleeding and cut up, his hair as tangled as a bird's nest.

Finally, Atticus raised his gaze to look at his son—but only for a moment, before he looked down again.

I imagined how humiliating this must be for him.

Lawrence moved stiffly toward us, his eyes trained on his father.

"Lawrence," I said brightly. "You've arrived just in time. We've been discussing what we ought to do with your father but, really, I think that is a decision that should be left to you."

Given Atticus's responsibility for the murder of his mother, that seemed to be only right.

Lawrence breathed in through his nose, his lips pursing as he gazed at his father with deep disdain. There was a pause of a few minutes as he circled him silently.

Finally, Lawrence's lips parted and he spoke in a deep voice. "I think I know exactly what we ought to do with you, Father... It's about time you face the public."

LAWRENCE

After witnessing my father captured in our midst, and arriving at an idea for what to do with him, I requested Ibrahim to heal my aching shoulders and the gash in my cheek, which he did without much delay.

Then I looked around at our group.

"Does anybody know if the news sites and channels are up and running again?" They ought to be by now, but I needed to verify it.

"They are," Ben confirmed.

"Then I suggest that we go and pay a visit to those news helicopters."

I couldn't help but look at my father as I spoke. His jaw was tight, his teeth clenched, his cheek muscles twitching.

Kailyn and Ben continued to grip him as they began flying toward the helicopters, while I returned to Jez. Sofia and Derek flew with their dragon. Given the presence of the dragon and the mutant, the news reporters were unsurprisingly jittery to see us come hurtling toward them.

The helicopters began to move away, and Derek had to ask the dragon to use his mighty voice to bellow out, "We are here only to talk!"

That made them stall and hover where they were, waiting for us to approach. Jez and I reached the nearest helicopter first, and I leapt into the belly of the aircraft, leaving the mutant to hover outside. Derek and Sofia joined me, followed by Kailyn, Ben and my father.

The helicopter was filled with at least ten reporters, and I could recognize from their badges and dress that most of them represented the major channels.

As famous—or should I now say, infamous—as the IBSI was, my father himself was practically invisible to the public eye. He almost never showed his face, and most people had no idea who actually ran it.

They did, however, recognize me, given my numerous appearances on the screen as the IBSI's "golden child" and test-experiment-gone-wrong. Their brows rose as they laid eyes on me.

"This is my father, Mr. Atticus Conway," I said, gesturing toward him. "Founder and chief of the IBSI, if you weren't aware. I would like you to set up your cameras now. My father has some confessions to make."

The reporters set up the cameras and pointed them at my father and me. Then they began to record. My father's face had flushed red as he kept his head down, still refusing to look at me.

I looked directly at the cameras and gave an introduction to myself before moving on to introduce my father. "This is the man who is responsible for every activity the IBSI has carried out since its founding. He is the IBSI's founder and director. Until now, he has lurked in the shadows of the organization's halls, but now, I would like to introduce him to the world."

I paused to address my father. "Do you have anything to say at all?"

He remained silent. That was about the only act of protest he could pull off in this moment.

"Well, it seems that Mr. Conway is speechless," I went on. "Allow me to introduce him further. He is the murderer of his wife, my mother, Mrs. Georgina Conway, who died thirteen years ago in a covert assassination. Since then, he has assassinated many other innocent members of his organization. What was their crime? They wished to spread the knowledge about the Bloodless antidote far and wide to the public." I had already explained several hours earlier when we were visiting news stations about the cure and how it had been concealed in order to provide an excuse for the IBSI to remain in power. Of course, we had demonstrated the antidote too. But I recapped it now in brief for any who had not watched the previous broadcasts or seen the viral footage on the internet.

I turned once again to my father. "Do you deny any of this?"

I expected him to maintain his silence, so I was surprised when he responded in a deep, coarse voice. "You speak the truth about many things, but not about my intent." His blue eyes pierced through mine. "You should have gleaned by now, Lawrence, that power has never been my or the IBSI's motivation. Power has always been a means to an end. An end which is for the benefit of all mankind. Given the state that the world is in, and has been in for the past several decades, drastic measures have been required in order to keep human society from descending into irrelevance." He went on to clarify why they had kept the antidote such a closely guarded secret; they needed it to retain control, and they needed control in order to change the world for the better, develop a new breed of humans who would be powerful enough to withstand supernaturals. "We've had to think about safeguarding our future," he concluded, "and for that, sacrifices needed to be made."

Derek cleared his throat. "That's all well and good," he said, glaring daggers at my father. He looked toward the cameras to address the public. "But you will witness in the days, weeks, months and years to come that Mr. Atticus Conway's methods, however *noble*"—here, Derek's voice dripped with sarcasm—"are not required. There are ways of dealing with Earth's situation other than keeping hundreds of thousands of people living a life of sheer misery. Not to speak of murdering innocent people."

If my father's hands had not been bound, I was sure that he would've punched Derek. But now that he had practically confessed to these matters on television, my father's hands would be cuffed for a long time to come.

"I cannot say that I am sorry for anything." My father spoke to the camera. "And if you trust a word that comes out of Derek Novak's mouth, you're fools. TSL will bring this country, and the international community, to ruin. Their efforts will not sustain the way the IBSI has for decades. You'll see, all of you. Every single one of you will suffer if the IBSI is overthrown."

"Not *if*, Father," I said, raising a brow at his choice of words. "When." In fact, it had already happened. Just not officially yet.

I told the reporters they could stop filming—I figured that they'd captured enough of our banter, and since my father obviously wasn't going to apologize for anything, I didn't see the point of going on.

As I turned to speak to Derek, my phone rang in my pocket. Thanks to my pockets having zippers, it had survived the fall from the building. I took the call and pressed it to my ear.

"Lawrence." It was Fowler. "Hand the phone to your father, please."

I held the phone to my father's ear, my pulse quickening.

Even though it wasn't on loudspeaker, I could make out Fowler's voice on the other end of the line.

"You are going to have to step down," Fowler said. "Henceforth, the IBSI is disbanded."

My father's lips cracked open, but in that moment he looked too furious even to talk. Heck, he looked like he wanted to throw himself out of the helicopter. I actually would not be surprised if he resorted to suicide after this. His whole life had been dedicated to the cause of the IBSI, however twisted it was. He'd sacrificed his wife, his son... Everything that should've been dear to him, he had placed on the line for his organization. I wasn't sure what else he had left to live for after this.

That appeared to be all Fowler wanted to say. I removed the phone from my father's ear.

"Make sure your helicopter stays where it is," Fowler said. "Police officers are heading your way now as we speak… No doubt, we will talk again soon." With that, he hung up.

I was surprised that he had not asked to speak to Derek about TSL's taking over now that the IBSI was disbanded. I wondered if it was his ego delaying the conversation, the fact that he would need to eat humble pie. From what I understood, the last words Fowler had exchanged with Derek had been Fowler "firing" him. Plus, it was clear that TSL was already inclined to take up the role of the IBSI—it was hardly like we were waiting for their permission. So maybe he thought he could afford to drag it out longer.

The police aircraft arrived swiftly. It closed the distance between itself and our helicopter before men laid down a ramp to connect their aircraft to ours.

As two burly policemen crossed the ramp, Ben and Kailyn relinquished their hold on my father and pushed him toward the men, who grabbed him by the arms.

My father twisted around one last time to look at me. I wasn't sure what I saw behind those cold blue eyes of his. It was hard to tell whether there was even a flicker of remorse—genuine remorse—behind them. He mostly seemed deeply dismayed.

I couldn't bring myself to care what he thought anymore. He would be placed behind bars and then the nation's judicial system would decide what fate lay in store for him. Perhaps he would be given the death sentence.

Whatever happened, as my father reached the police helicopter and the ramp drew away, the chapter of my life that he'd been a part of was closed.

DEREK

After Atticus was taken away, we left the press aircraft and headed to the ground. We finished sweeping through the city along with the rest of our army, until I felt comfortable that we'd searched as thoroughly as we could to find any surviving humans. All those we'd found were transported by witches back to The Shade's hospital.

Next, I set my eyes on the IBSI's Chicago HQ in the distance. Although TSL still had not received an official transference of authority, Fowler had basically said as much. I was still waiting for his call—I knew it would come. He would have no choice but to speak to me, sooner or later.

For now, I headed with Ben, Sofia, Lawrence, Aiden, Ibrahim and twenty other witches to the IBSI's compound. The army the IBSI had sent out to fight us had been so big, I doubted there would be many people left in the buildings, or at least none of the dangerous ones.

But even if there were fighters hanging on in there, they must've known what had been going on out here. They would've been monitoring the news, they would've seen the destruction. I didn't expect much trouble storming the hallways.

The IBSI members we found in the buildings were helpful in navigating the place. We stormed inside, passing through room after room informing whatever men and women we came across that the IBSI was shutting down. Nobody had made any promises to me that TSL would inherit the IBSI's buildings, but I didn't care. I was going to claim them.

We informed those left of their choice—leave here forever and find another job, or join forces with TSL. Most we came across opted for the latter, again demonstrating Jennifer Thornton's suspicion regarding many of the IBSI members to be correct. Most were loyal to power, whoever held it. And to whatever entity would keep themselves and their families safe.

Once we had scoured the base, essentially marking it as

ours, we returned to the entrance of the compound.

I left Aiden in charge along with Ibrahim and ten other witches. I needed Aiden and Ibrahim to start making the facilities suitable for TSL's purposes, and induct our newly joined recruits into TSL's way of thinking and behaving. That might take a while for them to get used to, given the years of brainwashing they must've received in the form of training under Atticus's organization.

As for the rest of us, we headed back to the city. I climbed atop Neros, who barked out orders on my behalf for our entire army to gather, something that took a while. Many of the werewolves and ogres had wandered far off in their search for stray humans (or Bloodless). But eventually, everyone had gathered.

I started by congratulating them on completing our first milestone successfully. Then I explained the second stage of our plan.

Our next stop had to be New York and Los Angeles. We could not travel there one at a time; we had to hit the two at once because we couldn't afford to waste any more time.

I split the army roughly in half, except for the dragons. Those I would send to New York, given their reluctance to travel by magic.

Lawrence and Ben headed one group, bound for New York, while Sofia and I headed the other, bound for Los

Angeles.

The dragons shouldn't be required anyway, except as a convenient means of flying. I didn't see the remaining stragglers of the IBSI as a threat anymore. Currently our main priority was to deal with the Bloodless streaming through residential areas, work on curing them with the large batches of antidote Dr. Finnegan had managed to create, and save the humans who had not yet been touched.

I was thankful that the IBSI had not pulled down more walls, though I reminded myself that there were still many IBSI leaders running rampant. They would be seething mad. I expected out of spite they would pull down more walls before our job was done, and if they did, so be it.

We just had to be as fast as we possibly could. We had to work for as many days or weeks as it took to infiltrate every single IBSI base in America and take it over. Fix what was broken, convert the hunters to TSL's side, and install leaders there who could begin training the men and women, and managing the operations.

And so began our journey.

When we arrived in Los Angeles, the city was in hardly any better state than Chicago. The Bloodless were running amok. It took us a full day to regain some semblance of order, all the while keeping in regular contact with Ben and Lawrence to check their progress in New York. By the sounds of it, New York had been an even worse mess. But once both cities had been re-organized, management put into place, and a deadline set for when they would aim to cure the last of the Bloodless that had been roaming the city, we moved on to other areas. And in doing so, we had to split our army up further for the sake of speed. It was a good thing I had gathered up such a large one. We needed as much manpower as we could possibly get. And equally as fortunate was the fact that Dr. Finnegan, with the help of a team of witches, had managed to mass-produce the antidote.

At least, the more cities we visited, the more IBSI members we gathered to help us. They proved to be invaluable since they knew the facilities inside out. We also trained them in administering the cure, which sped up the process further.

All the while, we were followed by the press. We encouraged them to film and snap pictures as much as they wanted. Let the world witness how we were curing the Bloodless, rather than slaughtering them… or deliberately creating more of them. There would be no secrets behind TSL's doors.

By the time I'd finished touring the states, spending as much time as I thought necessary in each area, overseeing and providing guidance to the managers we had appointed, almost a month had passed. Almost a month of practically no sleep, and very little nutrition. I wouldn't have been able to do it if I was a human. Even as a vampire, it was starting to take its toll. Sofia had remained traveling with me, and she was just as exhausted as I was. I had hardly seen my son, daughter, or the rest of our family and friends, because we were mostly scattered in different parts of the nation, each with our own responsibilities to fulfill.

Over the weeks, I did speak to several government officials (though still not Fowler). They informed the former employees of the IBSI that TSL was officially replacing them, and if they wanted to keep their jobs, they'd need to join us.

Finally, I felt that we had made enough headway to allow ourselves to withdraw at least for a few days—head back to The Shade to recuperate before returning and resuming our management duties.

As for Atticus, he'd come down to Earth with a crash. No longer an "untouchable", according to the news we heard during our travels, he'd been sentenced to a lifetime in jail. He should have been sentenced to death, but the authorities took into account the "service" he had performed over the years for the states and decided it was only right not to execute him. As twisted as he might have been, he had maintained some semblance of order in the country for the past couple of decades.

Something told me, however, that Atticus would have

preferred the death sentence. I wasn't sure what his purpose was for living anymore. He should probably avoid reading the papers or watching the news; it would drive him insane watching the "troublemakers" take over his empire. I would have liked to have watched him go through a more... physically painful punishment. But ultimately, I didn't care as long as I never had to see him again, and he never got another opportunity to cause trouble.

Sofia and I made one last round of the largest IBSI bases, where we gathered up our family and core TSL group. It was a relief to see everyone together again. I wasn't used to spending so much time apart.

Every bone and muscle in my body ached. I wanted nothing more than for Sofia and me to lock ourselves in our penthouse, collapse into bed and sleep.

Some dragons said that they would also return to our island for a break, and as for the rest of the supernaturals, provisions were made for them around the cities themselves, set aside from the humans. We had been sure to station ample witches in each place to keep an eye on the ogres—and assist with the general proceedings. However, I had to admit that the ogres were doing a commendable job. We truly were proving Atticus wrong in every single respect of his declaration that supernaturals were incapable of taking responsibility and becoming guardians to Earth. His convoluted idea that the IBSI was the only way to bring about peace again in the world.

So far, our focus had been primarily on the Bloodless; we hadn't even started to hunt down the other kinds of troublemaking supernaturals. That would be our next step. On paper, the supernaturals we'd brought down had no responsibility for the Bloodless; the Bloodless weren't members of the supernaturals' own species. Yet they were working to help us get a handle on them. I was sure when the time came they would do a diligent job of keeping their own kind in check, too.

We made Chicago our final port of call, where we prepared to finally leave for The Shade. But as we gathered together outside the former IBSI, now TSL HQ, a crowd of press reporters approached. Their eyes were trained on me specifically as I faced them.

"Sir, would you mind answering a few questions?" a thin woman with a short bob of blonde hair asked, clutching a mic in her hands. Miss Porter, according to her badge.

I let out a sigh. "Go ahead."

"Do you have a timeline for the Bloodless treatment?" she asked, moving the microphone beneath my chin. I clasped it and cleared my throat.

"As yet, I am uncomfortable about giving a timeframe. But rest assured that we have men and women working around the clock to administer it as fast as possible, in as many places as we can. We will also be introducing training programs to members of the public who wish to volunteer to help us speed up the process."

"Many are expressing concerns about your supernatural workforce. How can we trust they won't turn on us?" a male reporter asked.

"They will earn your trust," I told him firmly. "You cannot paint all supernaturals with the same brush. Just as you cannot with humans."

Dozens more questions were thrown my way regarding our methods and plans, until finally I had to put a stop to it and call for two last questions. My group was exhausted and it wasn't fair to hold them up like this. We could hold a large press conference in a few days' time.

"Where do you plan to go now, Mr. Novak?"

"Home, for a few days of rest."

"Will The Shade remain your home, even with your newly appointed duties?" the blonde-haired woman asked.

At this, I couldn't help but smile. "Yes, Miss Porter. No matter how far away my duties take me, or for how long, The Shade will always remain my home."

GRACE

The last month had been a mixture of awe, relief, and excitement for me, as I witnessed from afar, via the news and frequent updates from my father, what TSL and their massive new army had been doing.

And Lawrence. My heart swelled with pride for him, the way he had thrown his life on the line to bring down his father's corrupt reign. My eyes filled with tears as I imagined how proud his mother would've been if only she had still been alive. He'd made sure that she had not died in vain. He had taken up her beacon and carried it the final all-important stretch. The world would never be the same again because of what he and all of our people had accomplished.

I wished that I could be there alongside them, but since I couldn't, once I was allowed out of the hospital, I spent as much time assisting Dr. Finnegan and her team in mass-producing the antidote as I could.

When I wasn't helping her, I was usually with Orlando and Maura, my mother, Aunts Lalia and Dafne, Grandma Nadia, and Field—glued to the news. My cousins Hazel and Benedict also joined us often—Benedict was making an extra effort to not be annoying to me. (He was actually showing a lot of concern for my recovery, which I found cute.)

Things had been a hundred times less awkward between Orlando and me since he had rediscovered his sister. She had filled a gap in his life, taking the pressure off me. I still caught him gazing at me in a way that I wished he wouldn't from time to time—I supposed he couldn't help himself—but he was happy now. He was genuinely happy.

As was Maura. She had been in a much worse state than I had been after returning to her human form. The recovery had been much slower and more painful because she had been a monster for longer than I had. But she was making steady progress.

I hadn't exactly known Maura long before she'd gotten separated from Orlando and me in Bloodless Chicago and turned into one of them. Even during the short period we'd spent together, I couldn't exactly say that we had gotten on like a house on fire—she would have turned me over to the IBSI at one point if it hadn't been for Orlando persuading her otherwise. But since she had been cured, it felt like we had started a new chapter. We got to know each other afresh, without the strains that dystopian Chicago had laid upon us. She was much more relaxed, no longer snappy or moody as she had been. More than anything, she was just filled with relief and gratitude that she had been saved.

I could relate to that feeling. As for my own recovery, my hair was slowly growing back, I had put on weight, and my nails were also developing and strengthening. Although I was kept on a strict diet and medication routine to ensure that I healed as fast and thoroughly as possible, two weeks after TSL left the island I was allowed to go home with my mother. This was thrilling to me.

Orlando chose to stay in the hospital with Maura, since she still had some way to go. Field and the other boys were housed in a spare mountain cabin. They expressed their desire to stay together, and so we put them up in one of the five-bedroom homes.

Field ended up spending a lot of time with my mother and me at home, allowing us to discover more about his personality—something that appeared to be almost as much of a discovery process for him as it was for us. All he'd ever really known was struggle. He'd never had much time for recreation, discovering likes and dislikes. He'd lived each day in survival mode, doing anything and everything he could to survive.

Although we were often going in different directions during the day, we made a point to always meet for mealtimes. Field sometimes brought along his brothers to join us.

Victoria and Bastien also returned with Mona and Brock, which was a treat. I spent some quality time with Victoria, catching up on the crazy adventure she'd been through, causing my mouth to hang open. I could hardly believe that she was married now. Married! And to Bastien. We had hardly seen each other recently and her returning with this news seemed so sudden. Apparently she had already told her parents about it.

I didn't see a lot of her after our initial catchup; I guessed that she was busying herself with Bastien. Starting a new life with someone was no light matter.

When my father called one evening and finally told us of their plans to return, I could hardly contain my excitement. I missed everybody so much, especially Lawrence. It felt like an eternity since I'd last seen them. So much had happened. So much had changed.

They were due to return the next evening, and that night

after the call ended, I could hardly sleep. The next morning, the only thing on my mind was their arrival, and I found myself leaving Dr. Finnegan's side late that afternoon to begin preparing myself for their return.

I was holding out hope that they might even arrive earlier and I wanted to be waiting at the Port when they did. After taking a quick shower, I found myself in my bedroom, gazing at myself in the mirror and examining the progress my body had made. My hair was short and spiky, a look that I disliked, to say the least. Short hair didn't suit me in general, and definitely not this short. One of the jinn had created a wig for me that looked incredibly realistic, but most days, I hadn't bothered to wear it. Now, however, at the thought of seeing Lawrence again, I experienced a bout of self-consciousness. I decided to put the wig on before applying some light makeup to make me look healthier and give myself a boost of confidence.

Then, although evening had not yet arrived, I headed to the Port with my mother. We sat on the edge of the jetty, gazing out at the ocean as we waited for our loved ones to return. Hazel and Benedict joined us, seating themselves and dangling their legs over the edge beside us.

My mother glanced at me and smiled. She squeezed my hand.

"How are you feeling?" she asked.

I blew out softly. "Lighter than I've felt in a long time," I told her. "I just can't believe we've managed to come this far, when so many odds were against us. It feels surreal."

My mother's eyes twinkled. "It does feel surreal. But justice has a habit of finding a way… And by the way"—her smile broadened—"I don't blame you for falling for Lawrence. I think you've really found yourself a catch in that young man."

I smirked, my cheeks warming. After Lawrence's recent transformation, he was an undisputed hottie. It wouldn't be difficult for any girl to fall for him. But I had fallen for him before that, when he'd still been a sickly boy bound to a wheelchair, barely even able to shave himself. I'd fallen for him deeper than I'd even known at the time. When he'd been taken away from us by his father, his absence had created a void in me. And it was that void that had spurred me to follow Georgina's trail and discover her secrets.

Lawrence had gotten a chance to test how deeply he felt for me, too. I hadn't noticed any difference in his eyes when he looked at me while I was a sickly, frail thing than when I had been normal and healthy. I felt that he loved me without condition, as I loved him.

"Lawrence is awesome," Hazel commented, giving me a wink. And at this point, I knew Benedict wouldn't be able to help himself from weighing in, too.

Seated on the other side of his sister, the kid dipped his face forward to look at me. He raised his brows warningly. "I hope you've made the right choice."

I raised my own brows. "Why do you say that?"

"Well, once you get with Lawrence, Heath will be off the table."

I snorted. "Oh, I see. Well, leaving aside the fact that Heath has been off the table for a while, warning noted... But don't you approve of Lawrence?"

Benedict pursed his lips. He leaned back on his hands and stared out at the ocean, giving it a moment's thought. "Yeah, I guess so," he muttered eventually. "He is kind of badass."

Hazel and my mom giggled, while I let out an exaggerated sigh of relief. "That's good to hear, Benedict. I'm not sure what I'd do without your approval."

After that, the four of us fell into mostly silence, waiting in electric anticipation. We watched the sun beyond the boundary sink lower and lower in the sky, until evening decidedly set in.

About half an hour later, finally, they returned.

The large group of our closest friends and family manifested on the beach, about thirty feet away from us. The four of us shot to our feet and dashed across the sand toward them. My father, standing near the front of the crowd, was the first to reach my mother and me, while Hazel and

Benedict darted toward Rose and Caleb.

My father was practically strangled by my mother's and my dual embrace. He held us tight, wrapping one arm around our waists and kissing our cheeks. Next, I was scooped up in a bear hug by my grandfather Derek. He kissed my forehead before allowing my grandmother Sofia to embrace me. Next I greeted Uncle Jamil, Aunty Rose and Uncle Caleb. Then came my great-aunt and uncle, Vivienne and Xavier, and then my great-grandfather Aiden and Kailyn.

As I milled through the sea of faces, greeting the rest, my eyes were wide on the lookout for Lawrence. I still hadn't spotted him. It was only once I'd reached the back of the crowd that I found him in conversation with Ibrahim. A conversation that stopped short the second Lawrence laid eyes on me.

He looked exhausted, hair disheveled, stubble overgrown, and yet more handsome to me than I'd ever seen him. His tawny brown eyes lit up, his lips breaking out into a smile.

Ibrahim took his cue to leave. He moved passed me, squeezing my shoulder and expressing his relief that I was all right, before following the rest of the crowd who were making their way to the mainland.

It was just Lawrence and I left behind.

I launched into his arms. My arms locking around his

neck, I pulled myself up against him while his hands clutched my waist. I buried my face against his shoulder, warmth rolling through me as his lips found the bare skin at the base of my neck. My chest tight with emotion, I breathed, "I missed you so much."

His hands moved up my back as he drew us apart enough to take in my face. His eyes had gone glassy. They roamed my face, taking in every detail of me, before settling on my hair. Or rather, my wig. A slight frown twitched his brows.

"Your hair didn't grow back that fast, did it?"

I shook my head.

His fingers reached into the base of my scalp. He'd found the base of the wig.

"I hope you didn't put that on for me?" he asked, still frowning.

I bit my lip. It would have been a lie to say that I hadn't. He read my expression.

Tugging at the wig's base, he gently removed it. He studied me again, even as I felt bare.

He leaned down and closed his lips around mine in a slow, tender kiss. Then his lips trailed across my cheek, moving to my right ear while his arms resumed their hold around me, pulling me flush against him. "Don't try to change for me, Grace. I want you as you are."

As he kissed me again, I melted into him, all inhibitions

falling away. I forgot time and place. The sand beneath our feet. The wind in our hair. The calm lapping of waves against the shore. As our embrace intensified, passion coursing through our veins, I could just about manage to whisper, "You're my hero, Lawrence."

Sofia

As soon as we left the beach, Derek and I headed to our treehouse. With the thought of our soft, warm bed, my eyelids were practically drooping as we ran. We entered the apartment and plodded to the bathroom like zombies, where we stripped and took a quick shower before arriving in our bedroom and falling into bed. I cuddled up next to Derek, my head against the crook of his neck, and within a few minutes, sleep claimed us both.

I ended up sleeping for eighteen hours straight. That was a bizarre thing for a vampire. But we both needed it. It would

A DAY OF GLORY

take us a few days of extra sleep before we felt our normal selves again after so much sleep deprivation. We could have slept in the residential quarters of the various former IBSI bases, but while we were away neither of us could bring ourselves to get any real sleep, even though we tried. There was simply too much to be done in that crucial takeover period, and Derek and I needed to be hands on every step of the way.

As I woke up at a few minutes past one PM the following day, Derek was still asleep. I managed to extricate myself from his hold without waking him and headed to the bathroom. After brushing my teeth and taking a shower, I was about to head to the kitchen when my phone buzzed on the coffee table in the living room. I checked it to see a text message from Vivienne.

"*You two awake yet?*"

I phoned her back. She picked up after two rings. "One of us is awake," I informed her throatily.

"Hope I didn't disturb you."

"Nah. What's going on?"

"Xavier and I are in the process of arranging a proper wedding for Vicky and Bastien. I know that's probably the last thing you want to hear," she added, "but it won't be a big affair. Just something low-key and uncomplicated. Neither of them want anything fancy."

"On the contrary," I said, beaming at the thought of my niece in a wedding dress. "A wedding sounds like the perfect way for all of us to unwind."

We only planned to rest here for three days, and we needed to make those days count by relaxing as much as possible and distracting our minds with anything other than work. If we didn't unwind fully, we wouldn't be rejuvenated when we returned to our duties.

"When will it be? Do you need help with anything?"

"We're planning it for this evening, at five," she said. "And no, we don't need help. Corrine's already sorted the dress with us. Just turn up at the Port. It'll be a beach wedding."

"Sounds good," I said, smiling against the phone. "I'll make sure your brother is up by then."

I hung up and padded to the bedroom. When I peered inside, Derek appeared to be stirring, or at least not sleeping as heavily as when I'd left. I approached his side of the bed. Kneeling down, I gazed at his peaceful sleeping face. Derek looked cute when he was asleep. When no frown was marring his forehead, no intense blue eyes to contend with. He looked innocent… almost.

I leaned closer and kissed his forehead. As I was about to move away and leave the bedroom to allow him to continue to rest, his arms shot out abruptly and wrapped around me.

The next thing I knew, he was pulling me down on top of him.

"Derek!" I laughed as he pulled me beneath the sheets with him and slipped them over our heads. His eyes opened with a mischievous gleam.

Not so innocent…

"You were on the phone to Vivienne?" he asked, his voice husky.

"Yes. We've got a wedding to attend at five. Your niece's."

Derek rolled over on his back, still keeping one arm wrapped around me like a snake. He ran his other hand down his face. "Wow. I feel old."

"All of five hundred and… fifty-something years?" I asked. "Yeah, even I've lost track."

He sighed.

"Promise me you'll force yourself to relax for the next two days," I told him, brushing my fingers through his hair.

"Yeah. I will."

I pulled him out of bed, into the bathroom, where I ran a bubble bath. After Derek had shaved his stubble, we slipped into the bath tub together. Sitting behind Derek, his back against my front, I had fun piling handfuls of stiff foam onto his head and fashioning a new, comically square hairstyle. When he'd had enough of me doing that (with the complaint that I was dripping bubbles into his eyes), he brushed away the foam with one hand and switched positions with me. Then things got a little more... heated. It had been more than a month since we'd had quality time together, and we hungered for each other.

Next we dried off and retreated to our bedroom to get dressed. After blow-drying my hair—and Derek's—I slipped into a light lilac gown, while Derek pulled on a tuxedo. I loved it when he wore a tux. He looked like such a gentleman. It was nice to have a change from the bloodstained, torn-clothed warrior once in a while. Derek in a tux reminded me of our wedding day, and even as he stood before me now, his back turned to me as he adjusted his bow tie in front of the mirror, I felt my heartbeat quicken.

I grinned at his reflection. He caught my eye, my smile spreading to his face. "What are you looking at?" he asked.

"What does it look like?" I countered, slipping behind him and wrapping my arms around his waist. "My slick husband."

He smirked and finished adjusting his tie before turning to face me. His eyes roamed my own outfit briefly before he planted a kiss against the side of my neck. "You could wear your nightgown and I'd hardly notice."

"Yeah, I know," I said, sliding my arms around his midriff. I narrowed my eyes teasingly. "Because you're too lost in my eyes, right? Not because you're a typical guy."

Derek pulled a deadpan expression. "You'd call me cheesy if I admitted the former."

"Oh, come on, Derek. You're already a cheeseball." I pulled his head down and closed my lips around his. As his hands slid down to my waist, I smiled through our kiss. "A cheeseball if ever there was one."

Derek groaned contentedly as our lips kneaded. Then he broke away, his blue eyes fixed on me in a serious expression. "We'd better stop now, or I might need to readjust my tie..."

I let him step away. I suspected he'd have to do a bit more than readjust his tie if he let me have him again.

I moved to the mirror and did my hair before applying my perfume and a touch of makeup, while Derek returned to the bathroom to spray his cologne.

We still had a few hours before the wedding, but there was no harm in Derek and me arriving early to help set up. Weddings were always a public affair in The Shade, because we were all one big extended family. Although Vivienne had said they were planning to keep it low-key, there really was no such thing as a 'low-key' wedding in The Shade. Everyone was welcome to attend. That was one reason why we almost always held weddings outside, so there was enough room to accommodate as many people as wanted to show up.

Derek and I left our treehouse and took a leisurely stroll through the forest to the Port. On reaching the jetty, we glanced to our right along the beach to see some early arrivals. Xavier and Vivienne were setting up chairs and tables along with Corrine, Shayla and Arwen, who wore a light pink dress (which I suspected meant she was to be one of Vicky's bridesmaids).

My father and Kailyn were here too. They stood near the water, their feet submerged in the waves. My father was holding their newly adopted wolf baby—my new brother (that was an odd thought)—in his arms, while Kailyn cooed over the baby. As they sensed our approach and turned to face us, my father's and Kailyn's eyes shone with happiness. I was witnessing the baby in his humanoid form for the first time. His features made my heart melt. A perfect button nose; large, sparkling brown eyes. He was more hairy than a human baby—the mop of brown hair on his head was thick and lush, and his eyebrows were already pretty distinct.

I knew that my father would never want to have another biological child—he was past that stage of his life—and Kailyn had accepted that. Though as I saw how joyful she looked now with this baby, I sensed that she'd still harbored a desire for a baby. It was a good thing that we had visited that orphanage. Kailyn would make a wonderful mother, and I knew that my father would make a wonderful dad.

"Have you named him yet?" I asked.

"Uh, we're still mulling it over," my father replied,

exchanging a grin with Kailyn.

"Yeah," Kailyn said. "Naming a baby is a lot harder than I thought."

I lowered to plant two kisses against the infant's soft round cheeks. He reached out a small hand as I drew away. I placed my finger in his palm. His fingers closed around it with strength that surprised me… Though I shouldn't have been surprised. He was a supernatural. I just didn't have a lot of experience with werewolf cubs.

Derek and I moved away from the trio and headed to where the wedding was being set up. We approached Vivienne and Xavier, who were aligning instruments off in one corner.

They stopped working and looked up at us. I could instantly detect the nervousness in their eyes. Because I had been through all of this before with Derek. We knew what it was like to give a daughter away, even if it was to a man you trusted.

"How's everything going?" Derek asked, kissing his sister's cheek.

"Fine," she said, flashing a quick smile.

"Where's Vicky? How's she doing?" I asked.

"She's prepared already, and is waiting back in our penthouse. She wanted some time alone."

I caught a gleam of tears in my sister-in-law's eyes. She

averted her attention to the grand piano.

Derek gripped Xavier's shoulder and squeezed hard. "Now you know how it feels to give your baby girl away," he said.

"Yeah," Xavier said hoarsely, gulping.

Derek patted him on the back. "You'll get used to it. Even though it may seem like you never, ever will... You will."

Derek's words brought a smile to my lips. I remembered how cute he had been over that—when it came time to officially give our daughter away to Caleb. How melancholic he had been in the lead-up to the wedding. That had been a hard time for my husband.

On the subject of Rose, I spotted her walking toward us from the direction of the Port. She was with Caleb and my two grandchildren, Benedict and Hazel. Hazel wore the same colored dress as Arwen—bridesmaid number two, apparently.

Claudia and Yuri followed closely behind with their eighteen-year-old daughter Ruby, also in a pink bridesmaid dress.

As they approached, I kissed my daughter and son-in-law on the cheek before turning my attention to my beautiful granddaughter. Hazel wore a ring of daisies around her head, which had become slightly askew. I adjusted it and withdrew two pins from my own hair to keep it in place. It was hard to believe that Hazel would be sixteen soon. I still remembered the day she was born.

Then I stroked a hand through Benedict's brown hair. Benedict was looking rather dashing in a gray tuxedo.

Gratitude washed over me as I reflected on the family I had been gifted, a family that seemed to be growing larger with each year that passed. My heart felt like it was expanding with each new addition. When I was younger all I'd ever wanted was a family. My life now wouldn't have appeared in my wildest dreams back then. No matter what tough periods we had been through, they had always been surmountable because of my family. They were my support system. My life blood.

"Oh, look who it is," Derek said, pointing to the jetty.

Lucas was moving toward us with Marion, who was carrying her baby girl. Lucas had one arm around Marion as they walked, and he looked happier than I'd seen him in a long time. So did Marion. Apparently Claudia's trick to get the two to share an apartment had paid off.

Lucas's face flushed a little beneath our gaze as they neared. He seemed to be deliberately avoiding making eye contact with any of us. I thought he and Marion were adorable together. She clearly doted on him, and after many years of, ahem, maturing, I felt that Lucas would make a good man for her. The fact that she had a baby would force him to take on an extra responsibility—which I felt was a good thing to help ground Lucas.

This was the first time I was seeing my brother-in-law for quite some time. He hadn't come with us to America, which I didn't blame him for. He deserved a timeout after his misadventures in The Dewglades, though I suspected he'd come with us when we returned for our next round of adventures.

"How are you, dear brother?" Derek asked, clapping a hand against Lucas's back.

Lucas grinned rakishly. There was still a cute flush to his cheeks. "Haven't been better in a while, actually," he replied.

Cameron, Liana and their son Cedric, along with their daughter Poppy and Jeramiah, approached behind Lucas and Marion.

Then came Ashley and Landis with their teenage human son, Julian, followed by Mona and Kiev with Brock, Helina and Matteo, and Erik and Abby. They stood with us among the rows of seats, congratulating Xavier and Vivienne.

Ben and River arrived next. Grace and Lawrence walked behind them, hand in hand—Grace without her wig.

Shortly behind them walked Field and the other four Hawk-boys, and then Orlando, pushing his sister in a wheelchair.

As Claudia approached with Yuri, she threw Lucas a wink,

which he not-so-subtly tried to pretend he hadn't seen.

Kira and Micah strolled over with their new baby, Saira walking next to them with hers. All of the wolf cubs were in their humanoid forms now. Both looked as cute as Aiden and Kailyn's. They appeared to be siblings.

When Brett and Bella arrived from the direction of the caves, they were with the ogre babies they had agreed to take on. Brett carried the one who apparently had a thing for grabbing body parts—as it was trying to get hold of his ears and nose —while Bella carried the other, who was being a bit more well behaved. He sat in her arms, distracted by the crowd up ahead of them.

Bella and Brett still weren't officially a couple, though they were practically inseparable. They ate and roamed the island together, kept each other company in their caves; the only thing they didn't do was sleep together. I wasn't sure what was really happening, whether there was anything at all romantic going on between them, or if it was purely platonic. But if those babies didn't bring them together, I wasn't sure what would.

Speaking of babies, we still hadn't figured out what those odd gray scaly ones were. I suspected that we were going to have to take them to see The Sanctuary's witches to see if any of them had an opinion on the infants. Maybe we'd take one with us as a sample when we returned to America.

More and more people arrived on the beach as the next hour went by, until it was almost standing room only in the area where Corrine and her team had set up chairs. They had to magick more to accommodate everyone.

Yeah, so much for "low-key".

Finally, I caught sight of Bastien arriving. He wore a smart black suit, which I suspected Corrine had something to do with. He approached the raised platform that was bedecked with white flowers that Ruby, Hazel and Arwen were still putting in place. He climbed the steps and stood in one corner, gazing at the massive crowd. Bastien was still so new here to us in The Shade. I imagined how nervous he must be feeling to be surrounded by so many strangers. But he'd feel completely at home here soon enough. He was our family now.

Micah left Kira and his new baby son and approached Bastien, which made me happy. It seemed that Micah was going to be Bastien's best man. Ibrahim also made his way to the platform; he would be managing the formal proceedings, as he usually did whenever he was available.

We began to take seats. I moved to the front row with Derek and sat next to Vivienne, while Xavier made his way to the other end of the aisle to wait for his daughter.

As everyone settled down and we waited for Vicky, my daughter Rose started playing a soulful tune on the piano. I glanced at Vivienne. Her eyes were still glassy. I squeezed her knee, causing her to look at me.

"Everything is going to be fine," I assured her. I kissed her cheek.

Vivienne drew in a quick breath. "I know," she murmured, her eyes falling on Bastien. "I know."

Finally, the second star of the show arrived. Victoria approached the end of the aisle, her three bridesmaids Ruby, Hazel and Arwen carrying her trailing dress behind her. When she reached Xavier, she looped an arm through his. I couldn't see her face all that well beneath her veil, but I could make out enough of it to see that she was positively glowing. She looked so much like Vivienne in this moment it was breathtaking. The sight of her beginning to move down the aisle, about to enter a beautiful new phase of her life, reminded me acutely of the day Vivienne got married. Xavier's and her wedding... it truly seemed like an age ago. Ben and Rose had still been babies in my arms. My mind turned back to that glorious afternoon, so soon after we'd triumphed in ridding The Shade of the Elders. Xavier and Vivienne's special day was a memory I would never forget. That was also the day Ibrahim had proposed to Corrine.

Vicky reached the platform with her father. Xavier kissed her hand before allowing her to climb up to Bastien. As she stood before him, Bastien's cheeks shone with tears of happiness.

Ibrahim stood between them and conducted the usual proceedings. After exchanging vows and rings, Bastien raised her veil and drew his beautiful bride to him. When their lips locked, Vivienne broke down in tears.

Vicky tossed her bouquet into the crowd. There was a frantic scurry as our younger generation moved to snatch it. It was Hazel who emerged victorious, holding aloft the white roses. Her cheeks reddened as everyone sent wolf-whistles her way.

The formal ceremony over, Bastien and Vicky left the platform and headed to the dance area that had been set up by the rows of chairs, bordered by the group of instruments. They danced alone to a slow, romantic tune created by Rose, Shayla, and several other witches, before other couples began to join them.

Xavier took Vivienne's hand, while I made my way there with Derek. As I rested my arms over his shoulders and we began to sway, we shared a grin.

"Nostalgic much?" I asked him.

He nodded. "Yup. Every darn wedding."

I giggled.

As much as I could have lost myself in my husband's eyes for the next hour, I found myself gazing around at the other couples joining us. After three tunes had passed, many had started to make out. I nodded my head discreetly in the direction of Lucas and Marion, who oscillated near the border of the dancing area. Derek's chest shook as he chuckled. We quickly looked away as it seemed Lucas might notice us watching.

The lovebirds Grace and Lawrence also hung near the border, alternating between gazing into each other's eyes and kissing.

Brett's bellow punctuated the music at one point. When I gazed toward the noise, apparently he'd snapped at one of the misbehaving babies... They all sat on the ground near the food tables—which was where the ogres usually headed straight after any wedding. From where I stood, it looked like one of the babies had upturned his plate. Hopefully he and Bella wouldn't have second thoughts about adopting them.

Hazel swept past Derek and me, leading a rather lively dance with her twelve-year-old brother. I gazed over at the piano. Caleb had joined Rose in playing a duet.

"Oh, look. Theon's brought Penelope," Derek remarked.

I followed his gaze and, indeed, there she was. Her long dark hair hung over one shoulder, in a flowing green gown Queen Penelope Aena looked as regal as ever. Her face broke out in a smile as our eyes met. She stood with Theon, and Theon's brother Altair, who had also brought his ice dragon wife Merulina along. Lethe was behind them, holding hands with his pretty human wife, Elodie.

We moved to greet our latest arrivals, and by the time we'd returned to the dance, it was more packed than ever. Aisha, and her protruding stomach bump, whirled near us with her husband Horatio, while Anna and Kyle were lost in a world of their own behind us.

Weddings really were the best way to unwind. The stress of the last few months ebbed away as I rested my head against Derek's shoulder. So surrounded by everyone I loved and held dear, I felt full. Content. At peace with the world.

Even when I thought of our future now—like resuming our mission after our allotted three days were up—it was no longer with dread or fear. There was uncertainty, yes, because we were sailing completely new and uncharted waters. And of course, there would be obstacles. But I'd never felt so optimistic about the time that was to come. I was excited. More excited than I'd ever been. I couldn't wait to witness how everything would play out under TSL's new management, where supernaturals, for the first time in history, would become a mass force for good, rather than trouble. Working with us to root out evil, rather than cause it.

I suspected that this next stretch of the crazy journey that was Derek's and my life would be the most thrilling, rewarding and fulfilling so far.

The rest of the evening passed in a high of music, dance and laughter. Once it was time to cut the cake, Derek and I moved over to the food tables along with the rest of the crowd, but we stopped halfway. The phone in Derek's pocket went off. As he pulled it out and glanced down at the screen, a wry smile instantly curved his lips.

"It's Fowler," he said. "Finally." Gripping my hand, he led me away from the crowd and the noise, further along the empty beach. We stopped by the water, where he answered the call, putting it on loudspeaker.

His blue eyes were on me as he said, "Fowler?"

There was a pause before the man replied in a resigned tone, "Yes, Novak, it's me."

"About time," Derek replied tersely.

Another pause.

"I suppose I, uh, owe you an apology," Fowler said.

"Yes," Derek said, his dark brows rising. "I suppose you do."

"Well, you have it, Novak." As Fowler cleared his throat, there came another beat of silence. "I've been appointed your official point of contact again now that you're back on the job."

"Well, Fowler," my husband replied, "in case you didn't notice, I and my people were never actually *off* the job. Your 'firing' me didn't have even the smallest effect on our activities…

Because one can't simply fire a Novak."

IS THIS THE END OF THE SHADE?
NO, IT ISN'T!

There will be a Season 5!
Yay!

Dearest Shaddict,

Yup, that's right. Although the Season 4 story arc has wrapped in this book, you will be returning to The Shade very soon to reunite with your favorite characters in a brand new heart-pounding adventure!

Keep reading to learn about my *two* upcoming releases…

1st Announcement:
My non-Shade (and longest ever) novel

Check out the amazing cinematic trailer for my new novel **The Gender Game** by visiting my website: www.bellaforrest.net .

The Gender Game releases **September 24, 2016.**

If you have enjoyed the Shade books, here are **3 REASONS why you will love this book as well:**

1) <u>The Gender Game</u> has everything you've loved about the Shade: the mystery, the unexpected twists and turns, the **intense** romance… you will experience my signature writing style on every page.

2) It's the **longest** book I've ever written.

3) I can honestly say I believe this is also the best book I've ever written. I've never had a storyline possess me like this one has — the characters won't leave my head even when I sleep — and I've never been as excited to share a book with you.

This story is really something special and I hope you will give it a chance. I think you'll be pleasantly surprised :)

Visit <u>www.bellaforrest.net</u> for details on ordering.

Here's what early readers are saying:

*"Bella takes this genre to a new level. Imagine **the intrigue of Divergent, the suspense of The Maze Runner** and **the heart-pounding excitement of The Hunger Games**. That is the magic Bella is working with her new novel The Gender Game."*

*"The chemistry between the characters is **INTENSE**. Forbidden romance at its **best**!"*

*"You can **never** predict where Bella Forrest will take a story!"*

*"**Intrigue**, **danger** and **mystery** at every corner."*

And here's a preview of the spectacular cover:

2nd Announcement:
A Shade of Vampire 33: A Dawn of Guardians!

The next book in the Shade series, _A Shade of Vampire 33: **A Dawn of Guardians**_ is the start of "Season 5", a

brand new storyline. New romances to fall in love with. New mysteries to unravel. A new journey to lose yourself in.

Your Shade family is waiting for you in _**A Dawn of Guardians**_, releasing **September 14th, 2016!**

Pre-order your copy now and have it delivered automatically on release day.

Visit: www.bellaforrest.net for details.

Here's a preview of the gorgeous cover:

Thank you for reading.

I will see you again very soon!

Love,
Bella xxx

P.S. Join my VIP email list and I'll send you a personal reminder as soon as I have a new book out. Visit here to sign up: **www.forrestbooks.com**

(You'll also be the first to receive news about movies/TV show as well as other exciting projects that may be coming up!)

P.P.S. Follow The Shade on Instagram and check out some of the beautiful graphics: @ashadeofvampire

You can also come say hi on Facebook:
www.facebook.com/AShadeOfVampire
And Twitter: @ashadeofvampire